Becoming Queen Bathsheba

AMANDA BEDZRAH

EVELYN HOUSE PUBLISHING

Copyright © AMANDA BEDZRAH 2022

Evelyn House Publishing

ISBN: 978-1-8383044-5-4

Editor: Wendy H. Jones

Printed in the United Kingdom

This novel is a work of fiction, based on the Bible story in the book of 2 Samuel and should be read as such. There is no intention from the author to suggest this story is historical fact. Readers are encouraged to read the Bible.

Acknowledgments

A book like this cannot be written except by the grace of the Almighty God. Without Him, this book would only be a dream in my heart. I am thankful and truly humbled that God entrusted me with this story and gave me the courage to be firm in my convictions, to listen to His promptings as He whispered thoughts and ideas for this book.

I want to say thank you to my husband, Francois, and our three children. Your love and understanding enabled me to hide away many days and nights to write, your support and encouragement was the fuel I needed to keep going. I love you all so much.

I also want to say a huge thank you to my sisters, Efe and Eruke. Your consistent love and support are unrivalled. You girls make life so much easier, and you have been with me each step of the way, praying for this book, and listening to all my worries and concerns. Thank you so much.

To my dear girlfriends, you are my biggest cheerleaders. You know that I am so thankful for you all.

To my spiritual mums and mentors – Carol Bostock and Rev. Victoria Lawrence, your prayers and words of encouragement have carried me through this journey. I am forever thankful.

To every woman who has been deeply wounded, know that we serve a God of justice and restoration. He will give you beauty instead of ashes.

Prologue

c. 990 BCE Jerusalem
United Kingdom of Israel

As the sun fades in the sky, I sit rocking gently, gazing out of the vast window of the King's inner chamber and watching hints of orange flicker over golden brown clouds. My son suckles at my breast on this night before his first year on earth. The banquet room is already laid out: one hundred seats at the table, with the finest silver and gold plates, cups and cutlery at each place. The guests will arrive the early next day, travelling from near and far, some for days, honouring the King's invitation.

One hundred lambs were slaughtered earlier this day; the night is still thick with the fire from the smoke used to roast them in preparation for the morning. A seamstress arrived from Egypt more than a month ago, to sew the woven fabric for every royal in the house.

Though the sun is setting, the King is still on the throne, attending to matters of the nation of Israel. I am alone in his private quarters in the West wing of the palace. I look around me; the room is huge and quiet. How did I get here? I have asked myself this question at least a million times. Each time I try to think about it I am faced with painful memories. I paid a huge price for the crown that rests on my head. The more I think, the more I come to realise the cost, the pain, the sacrifice — the truth. Buried within my soul are words I have dared not speak or imagine; and yet, are dying to break free. Perhaps, someone somewhere may find comfort in my truth, in my journey, in my pain to becoming the woman I am today. It is for this reason I allow my mind to run freely today, closing my eyes and thinking back to three years previously, to the day it all began. I must remember, and I must write it down.

I place my son in the large woven basket filled with the softest wool blankets and equally soft cushions: I walk over to the large desk where paper and ink wait for me. I pick up the pen. I dip it in the ink. I apply it to the parchment. It is time to tell my story.

Chapter One

It has been many weeks since I last saw my husband Uriah, who was away in battle, fighting to protect the nation of Israel. Sadly, this was not the first time he had been gone for more days than I could count — a situation to which I never became accustomed. Many years ago, when we were first married, we had one glorious, uninterrupted year together. According to our custom, no man was sent to war or put to work during this time; a custom which allowed us to enjoy our time as man and wife. Our love grew deep.

As a trusted warrior for King David, Uriah has been in more battles than most other soldiers. One of the King's Thirty, chosen under oath and appointed by the King himself. This was one of the things I loved most about him. How ironic that the best part of him seemed to be the worst part — both a blessing and a curse! Uriah worked harder than all the others to be chosen as one of the Thirty. He had to. As a foreigner from the far region of the Hittites, he first had to prove himself loyal to our God, then to the Crown, and, lastly, to the people of Israel. It did not matter that he could swing the sword with ease and precision; it mattered more who it was pointed at, and it took him many years to establish the trust required to be accepted into the army of God, Yahweh as I fondly call Him.

I loved the way he loved his job. The pride in his face when he told me stories about the battles he fought, the places he visited, and the victories they enjoyed was always the highlight of his return. I enjoyed every minute of it hanging on his every word. These stories, good or bad, all fascinated me.

My grandfather Ahithopel, who I called Saba, was one of the King's chief advisors; my father, Eliam, was also one of the Thirty. So, I grew up hearing war stories and tales from lands far away. My mother, unlike me, did not like the war stories. I was different to most women all of whom detested the sight of blood or description of battle. I loved to hear every minute detail and Uriah spared nothing. He told stories in such a way that I felt I was riding a horse on the battle ground, in the middle of a war fighting for my life, hearing the clashing of swords and the cries of battle, the iron smell of spilled blood filling my nostrils. Fear clutched at my chest almost stopping my heart beating.

These stories were not always of victory. As with every nation there were instances of defeat, which meant periods of mourning followed. Those stories were the hardest to tell but still he told them, sometimes after he washed the taste of battle from his mouth with wine, through drunken tears. In those moments, I held him close and gave myself to him for comfort, the pleasure we shared as man and wife, a balm to his wounded soul. It was in those nights that I realised that even men of war, despite all the courage, valour, and strength they possessed, were weak in the bosom of a woman.

There were also times of mending wounds. I remember so well the first time Uriah came back wounded from battle. Oh, how I cried for days. A sword had sliced through his chest, barely missing his heart. It took many herbs, many physicians, and many months to heal. At various points I was fearful he would not heal and that he would leave to be with Yahweh.

Dare I share this secret? I'm ashamed to say I prayed for him not to heal quickly; and twice, maybe even three times, I put aside the herbs for strength and, instead, gave him the ones for sleep. This kept him weaker for longer. I wanted him home. I wanted him safe. I did not want him to go to battle again. I prayed he would be declared unfit for war and become one of the King's foot soldiers guarding the city gates. More than once I wished it was an arm the sword hit and not his chest. No one fought with a one-armed soldier, but I could be very happily married to a one-armed man. However, my prayers went unanswered. Please, don't judge me. I loved my husband; perhaps you can understand that — my willingness to have him safe and alive. The love within me burned far stronger than the satisfaction I got from the stories or spoils of war.

To my initial disappointment, he got better, much quicker than I expected and was on his feet eager to be back to the field. I did confess my sin to him, one night many months later. He told me, his voice stern, how disappointed he was. It cut deep as he looked away and spat on the ground to emphasise his displeasure, banishing me to the inner sanctum while he decided my punishment.

I made no sound as I waited in my own inner room as jumbled thoughts raced through my mind. It was not uncommon for a man to take a firm whip to his wife. While I dreaded this, I felt I deserved it. And if he truly wanted to, he could cast me aside and marry another. I rubbed my eyes with shaking fingers, attempting to stop my mind from darting in too many directions. I smacked my lips, cursing myself for sharing too much. Why did I do so? All it took was a few raisin cakes and one goblet of wine and my tongue was loose. Oh, why did I drink that wine? I did not have a head for it. Yet the stories seem so much funnier after a goblet of wine, even the ones when an enemy's head is chopped off, or when the weaker men beg for mercy. Although it was a mere few minutes that I sat in the room, banished like a naughty child, it felt like many hours had passed before I heard the door open and shut.

Uriah came to sit beside me quietly. "I have thought of a suitable punishment for you," he said through clenched teeth.

I wiped the water dripping from my forehead, with my scarf, before covering my mouth with my hand trying not to scream from the fear that boiled within me.

He turned and looked at me as I avoided looking at him, my eyes searching his hands for a whip or anything else he could use to hurt me. My skin was tender, having been brushed over and over for more than a week by the Egyptian slave my husband bought for me. She had prepared me for his return after hearing rumours from the town gate that a foot soldier had arrived at the palace a few days before to inform them to prepare for the King's return. Because of the brushing, anything Uriah did would bruise and hurt me. Please Yahweh, don't let him hurt me. My prayer flew heavenwards.

He must have sensed my anxiety as he cleared his throat to get my attention. "Your punishment is thus." His voice thundered. "No more wine, no more stories. You will stay up all night and please me; perhaps I can fill you with a child to keep you busy, so you don't miss me too much to want to kill me!"

Only then did I dare look into his eyes: the teasing smile that hung at the corner of his lips beckoned to me to draw closer. I let out a long sigh, and with a laughter louder than a respectable woman should exhibit, I eagerly slipped into his warm embrace. My Uriah! My love! How could I have ever imagined he would hurt me?

No sooner did the thoughts form in my mind than the words sprang from his lips: "I hope you had no fear that I would harm you!"

When I could form no words to respond, he could see the answer in my heart. He pulled me closer and whispered: "The only battles I fight are with the Lord's enemies; never in my own home. I swear by the God you serve, who gave me the strength I live by, that these arms will be to you only a shield and never a sword."

Then the night air was filled with the melody of love played by the bodies of two people playing a tune written in their hearts. Through his eyes, I had seen so much of life; through his words and actions I had heard and felt so much more.

Chapter Two

After that night there were many more wars in which he had to fight, meaning many more days of loneliness, followed by a few exquisite days of love and storytelling. Each time Uriah left, he left with a promise to return; and a hope that he had left behind a gift within me. He was always away when the disappointment came, the one that starts with a tug in the groin followed by days of bleeding. I think my disappointment was greater, but I cannot honestly say his was not as painful as mine. I saw it in his eyes each time he came home, especially when he had been gone for several months: and my stomach was as flat and empty as the day he left. He never gave up though, this husband of mine. He would hug me and remind me how much fun we would have trying once more.

He had told me his mother did not birth him until she was more than forty years old. But once he was born, she could not stop having children: she ended up with seven sons and three daughters. He did not know that that particular tale which he loved to tell, filled me with more dread than comfort. I was twenty-five years old, and the thought of having to wait fifteen more years tore at my heart and burned within my barren womb. I prayed this would not be the case for me. I was desperate for a child — his child. He was right. It would keep me busy and out of trouble; but it would also give me worth as a woman.

I started to live my days for the sounds of the trumpets. Although I busied myself with weaving baskets to trade, and learning how to weave fabric as well, I must honestly say it was waiting each day for news from war or the sounds of the trumpets that kept me waking up every morning. The triumphant blaring of trumpets always signified the return of the army, but it was the melody that it played that spoke volumes. By then, I had learnt the tunes by heart. The melody of victory rang in short, loud, continuous bursts. Then the drums would start to beat; and shortly after, loud screams of joy would erupt as women and children rushed out to welcome their loved ones home.

Then also, there was the trumpet that blew in short, sharp bursts; there were no drums: just a faint accompaniment of the harp, often played by the palace musicians. But on more than one occasion the harp was played by the King himself — a dirge, the sound of defeat. Instead of the screams of joy, there would be screams of sorrow and hours of panic and confusion as women searched for their husbands and mothers searched for their sons. Some heard news of their loved ones' death, while others welcomed husbands with broken bodies and often missing limbs. Those with only broken souls were considered lucky.

For all of the wars, I fell into the camp of the few lucky ones. I had no need to rush out to find Uriah. In fact, he had always told me never to join the mad rush regardless of the tune the trumpets played. Some people sustained injuries during the panic and confusion. Once, many years previously, a little boy had been trampled on: he did not survive it! Uriah insisted that he wanted to come home to me, whole or broken. He promised me by oath that if I waited for him, he would always come to me; and he did. Always.

Until the day he did not.

I was grateful that my grandfather Ahitophel not only had the King's ear, but he also had the King's trust. It meant I could often get the most reliable news far quicker than any of the other women. Not because my grandfather gave me an audience to discuss state matters. Far from it. But I knew that my servant Anushka had become his concubine. Saba was an honourable man by many standards, but he had a weakness for the taste and beauty of foreign women. It amused me each time Anushka lied to me that she heard word from a foot soldier. The first time, I believed her, until much later when I learned the truth. I will not bore you with the details of how I came to find out. I did not make a fuss as I had come to enjoy not just her hard work, but also her company. She was loyal to my household, and that mattered more to me than her indiscretion. Besides, I benefited more from their affair as more than once my words had reached my husband's ears even in the midst of battle.

Sometimes though, their affair came at a cost. Like that day, the one that changed everything. Anushka did not respond to my numerous calls. She had left the house unattended. The last seven days had been marked with sorrow as I washed away daily a reminder that my husband would return to an empty womb. Unlike the first few years of our marriage where hope filled his veins, it appeared that he had accepted for me, the fate of his mother. I was not willing to accept this for myself. I got out of bed and passed noon before I called Anushka again, longing for the warmth of honey tea to soothe me, as I dressed to go to the tent of the priest and then to the Mikveh, the communal bath required for ceremonial cleansing after the monthly period. For seven days, I had been ceremoniously unclean and set aside from everyone. Now on the eighth day I was required by our custom to take two young birds to the priest at the entrance of the Tent of Meeting for a sacrifice — one as a sin offering, and the other as a burnt offering to Yahweh. Most preferred to use doves as they were cheaper, but I chose to take pigeons as I had liked turtle doves ever since I was a little girl.

I chose to go close to sundown for several reasons: it was usually quieter as most of the men would have left the Tent of Meeting by then, the merchants selling sacrificial animals would have them at a cheaper price, and the Mikveh would be quieter.

I remembered thinking as a young girl just stepping into womanhood, how burdensome this whole process was. That first year was filled with many mistakes: I was careless and often made others in my household unclean. As the years passed, the rituals had now become second nature to me, although I did not like it. When I complained to my friend Salma, she would laugh and say, "A woman with child has nine months of no rituals, tell Uriah to fill your stomach." I wished it was that simple, that my word could carry such power.

Unconsciously, I rubbed my stomach. Then a wave of unexpected emotion swept over me, causing my eyes to water, I had just come out of niddah, so this was my most fertile time of the month. As I caressed my stomach I wondered — will it ever be filled? Will I ever be able to tell the stories of Yahweh to my own children? I was more learned than most women, always having had an interest in things that were considered more for a man. My curiosity led me to spend many hours listening at doorways while my male cousins were taught about our forefathers. I watched, crouched and hidden, as they learnt to scribe and even watched, surreptitiously, as they learnt to fight. That's how I learnt to do these things myself. I could both scribe and fight, something few women in the land could do. Yet, my fighting skills were useless in the face of the fiercest battle of my life. This battle was like none other. I found myself in the ring of life, in a field of war in which I could not fight, Whether I could wield a sword or use a sling or not was of no consequence in this war. I found myself helpless in the face of an invisible enemy — custom.

I did not even use my loud mouth that in my childhood, had often earned me a spanking from my mother, as I defended myself, enumerating every good reason I missed yet another cooking session or yet another fabric-mending session because I was climbing trees or spying on the boys as they learned to scribe. No, I did not use that voice. Not even the voice I dared to speak back to my husband more than once. Especially when I learnt that he took pleasure in the making up after a brief argument. No, I did not use that voice. Not because I did not want to, but because I could not. All available weapons were worthless in this invisible war in which I fought.

Because for the first time in my life, I found myself voiceless and powerless in the face of my culture and tradition. The one that knit the very fabric of our lives. The one that meant I am still alive to write my story. The one I've grown to hate. But I digress again. I must try to tell it in order. Where was I...? Aha, Anushka and the longing for tea!

Chapter Three

I walked towards the back of the house where the kitchen stood. It was fully stocked with everything that I needed. My husband's wages were more than enough to feed us, but we also got a portion of food and exotic spices straight from the King's palace: one of the many privileges afforded to the wife of one of the King's men. I quickly found the honey that I enjoyed most was from Persia. I do not know whether Persian bees ate a special diet different from other bees, but their honey was much sweeter.

I set the water jug on the warm coal, still cooling from the evening meal only a few hours ago and blew gently as I stopped to rekindle the fire. Soon, I had the hot water I needed to make a simple tea of water and honey into which I threw some raisins. If left for a few minutes, the raisins would swell up in the hot water and grow fat with honey, making an extra sweet treat to nibble on after drinking the tea. That was my favourite part as I enjoyed the snack even more than the tea. I must admit, I did not come up with the recipe, and you prob-

ably will not find it in any other households. It happened acci-
dentally one day when I dropped a piece of raisin cake in my
tea simply because I was talking and eating at the same time.
What annoyed me most is that it was the last bite as well. I
planned to savour it, but instead, I was forced to drink soaked
cake from my somewhat lukewarm tea. I do not mind admit-
ting that I grumbled slightly. Then I bit into the raisin: it was
like tasting heaven itself. That's how I started the
honey-raisin tea.

I carried my tea back into the living quarters and sat down
next to the open window staring at the sky. It was unexpect-
edly quiet; the sun was not yet asleep, but it was probably
yawning, getting ready for rest. I was alone. I felt alone. Why
did I not listen to Uriah when he told me to get more slave
girls?

The truth is, I had heard many stories of men taking their slave
girls as concubines. It was common practice, one that I wanted
to avoid in my household. I barely had enough of my husband
while he was home; even when not at war, he still spent a lot of
his time training in the palace or being the king's personal
guard when chosen to escort him to his numerous events.

I am not foolish enough to think my husband had never had
his fill of other women. There were some battles that they
returned from with not just gold and silver, but the wives and
children of the men that they defeated. Most times, the
journey home was long, and the soldiers were known to enjoy
the women as freely as they wished, using them as human
blankets in the cold dark nights. Uriah was a man like any
other; why would he not do as others did? I have no say in
what he does whilst away, but I knew I would be foolish to

bring slave girls into my own home. Anushka was an exception. She was much older than me. Not that her age impacted on her beauty in the slightest; if anything, it enhanced it. She was more like a big sister than a slave. So, this sudden loneliness borne out of my own selfishness was a small price to pay.

I looked out the small window as I decided to enjoy watching Yahweh's handiwork; the vast land that stretched before me was filled with monumental beauty. I took a moment to pray. My prayers usually had the same pattern: "Thank you Yahweh. Please protect your warriors in the field. Protect my husband and return him to me. Protect our nation and protect the King." That really was the extent of my prayers. At the time, I did not know how to pray for anything else. I did not even believe that I could. I had heard and learnt about Yahweh from the men in my household and mirrored their prayers. They always prayed for the nation and for the King. I did, however, add a special line for my husband, the man that I loved with every fibre of my being. I shivered slightly, a longing for him sweeping over me. I wrapped my arms tightly around my body as though in protection. I missed him dearly.

After waiting an hour more with no sign of Anushka, I dressed and hurried quickly to the Mikveh. I did not want to go to the Mikveh myself; I enjoyed Anushka's company, particularly her singing. Although the songs she knew were pagan songs, she had since learned to sing the melody without the words. She knew I worshipped Yahweh, the God of Israel, the One who had brought us out of Egypt with a great display of power.

I walked swiftly, weaving my way to the merchants. I bought two pigeons from a widow's son and hurried to the Priest and then on to the Mikveh. When I got there, I longed to undress and step fully into the freshwater bath which was rumoured to flow from the Gihon spring just outside the City of King David. Luckily, there were only a few women ahead of me. I sat outside on the cool green grass as I waited, looking around at not just the trees or the now sleeping sun, but also at the palace gates that stood far on the other side. They were majestic, high up in the sky as though they touched not only the clouds, but heaven.

I was lost in the beauty of the gates and my mind moved from my barrenness towards heaven, in prayer. Tears were forming in the corners of my eyes when Salma, a friend of many years, the wife of Malachi, one of the King's men, tapped me on the shoulder, reminding me to go in. Relief hauled me up from where my sadness almost kept me bound. I longed to be dipped and cleansed. There was something about the water swallowing me, that had a way of not just cleansing me in accordance with our laws, but also soothing me. It always created a perfect place to let my eyes leak with reckless abandon. It felt like the closest thing I could get to crying in the rain without actually being in the rain.

Even before I finished stripping off my clothes, my throat clenched tight from the struggle to stifle my sobs. I could almost feel an eruption of tears rumbling loudly in me. I did not know why I was so upset. It was just another month, like many others gone before. Why did my spirit feel so unsettled within me this month? Fear and many other thoughts of life and death slammed into me causing my chest to tighten. I coughed as my breath was caught in my throat. I started to question myself: surely by now I was used to not having my husband; where then did this fear come from? I knew it was fear. I have always known the taste of fear in my mouth. My mother never believed me when I told her I could taste my emotions. But I can. Why was I afraid? Deep down, I knew why: it was the same thing repeatedly. I may lie to myself on a regular basis, but deep down I knew exactly why. I was afraid that Uriah was right. I had another fifteen to twenty years to wait until I felt life swell within me or hear anyone whisper, "Mama."

Chapter Four

I released my long black and brown hair from the bun that had been packed neatly on my head the night before. My hair was thick, full, and fell all the way down past my waist. Anushka had spent many hours brushing it the day before, begging me not to trim it. I stroked my hair carefully, the same way I imagined I would have stroked my daughter's hair. It was then the tears almost blinded me with the fierceness with which they sprung. I needed air. Striding to the large window, I tossed it open.

The loud noise that seemed to come from a few houses down the road distracted me for a moment. I could hear music and laughter, but I could not see the merriment because the Mikveh had been crafted in a way that the bath quarter faced the opposite direction. It was deliberately built for privacy so no one could look in as women had to step in completely naked to be ritually cleansed. The Mikveh's window was positioned towards the stream and through it we could look up to heaven and recite our cleansing vows before we dipped in and, as we came out, thanking God for washing away our uncleanness. It was this large window I stretched my hand to open, drinking the night air I desperately craved.

Naked, alone and wet, I sobbed softly, taking my time to cleanse my body, staying under the water much longer than I needed to. As I emerged, I stood still and stared up to Heaven. This time, I wanted to pray differently but "Yahweh," was all I could say. All I could do was call on the name of my God through slightly parted lips. Then I tried to sing, just like Anushka. But Yahweh may have blessed me with a beauty that set tongues ablaze but not with the voice of a musician. When I sang, I scared myself. And I remembered scaring Uriah too. That made me chuckle. I laughed at the fond memory of my husband kissing me to silence me. It happened many years ago as we sat out in the cool evening under a sky full of stars. The heavens must have been having a festival because the sky was twinkling all over. There was also a full moon and the unusual sound of birds chirping in the dark.

We lay on a hand-woven rug made of fine sheep skin; it was very tender to touch. Uriah was perched on a huge cushion, leaning slightly to the left, partly because he had pain in his shoulders which was excruciating when lying flat, but also because he had a jug of wine he had been drinking from. It was then I did the unthinkable, I'm not sure why - I started to hum! It was a tune that was already playing by Mathias, the silver-smith that lived not many doors away from our own home. He was a master of metal but also a master of the flute. But I did not stop at humming. I started to sing. It was instant. No sooner had the words left my mouth than I felt the splash of the cold liquid on my right shoulder, the one that was leaning close to Uriah's chest. He spilled his wine in fright at the sound of my voice. We were never able to get the wine stain from that beautiful rug as it left a mark that morphed from red to deep purple over time and became a conversational topic for many visitors. My heart sang at Uriah's pleasure at telling that story at every opportunity.

The good thing about beautiful memories is that they warm the heart and can change sorrow to joy.

I came out cleansed and smiling, making a promise to myself to create more funny and treasured memories. I started planning the ways in which the next time I saw my husband, I would sing again. I realise now how foolish I was to think or dream of a future that would never come. In that moment, how was I to know I would never get a next time? Never!

Chapter Five

I had just dressed, after slathering my body and hair in the perfumed oils I had bought from the merchant just outside. It had cost much more than in the market square and I silently berated myself for forgetting to bring some of mine from home. If Anushka had been home, she would have attended the baths with me and she would have remembered the oils. I paid no heed to the fact I could not reach my back or that my hair was soaking and flying free; my thoughts were on hurrying home and falling into blessed sleep. Anushka could attend to me in the morning and perhaps I would get some word from the palace about the men at war. A few days ago, she had told me that the King had not gone to war alongside on this occasion. It was the talk of the town.

Although I chose not to indulge in careless whispers and mind-less gossip, I could not help but wonder why. It was my favourite time of the year - Spring. I loved the rich fruits, the cool weather, and the bountiful harvest. It was also the time when kings went to war! Why did King David not go? Instead, he sent Joab, his men including my husband, and my father and the whole Israelite army to war against the Ammonites.

I did not want to think about war that night. The images of the battle stories I relished hearing caused more pain than pleasure when the men were away. Living with the constant fear of their death was an almost unbearable burden. At times I felt my heart would break in two. Yet, as I looked up to Heaven, the only thing I could pray was, "Yahweh," and somehow, in that moment, it felt enough. I truly felt Yahweh heard my soulful plea.

It annoyed me greatly that the king sent his men to war while he stayed behind in his city. However, there was one good thing about his presence here — it meant there were frequent reports from the battlefield, more frequently than if he had gone himself. There were foot soldiers travelling back and forth every few days, bringing progress reports. I knew my husband was well and, for that news, I was grateful for the King's presence.

I stretched, and a loud yawn broke free leaping off into the silence of the night. The benefit of solitude - I could discard decorum at will. I even pressed my stomach gently to relieve the wind that swirled within me, gurgling like the child I knew I would one day have. I must drink some tea with mint leaves in the morning I reminded myself, fanning the air as though it would immediately disperse the smell.

I was shocked when I heard two loud knocks on my door! I knew I was the last to enter the Mikveh; the sun was falling fast asleep. Who could be knocking? And why? I was dressed now and just about ready to step out of the Mikveh into the road to my home. I had little fear of my safety, but I still approached the outdoor with caution, looking around for something to grab as a weapon. The only thing within reach was a water jug. I grabbed it and approached the door. "Who knocks?" I cried, my voice bolder than my heartbeat.

"Matthew. From the palace." He hesitated and added, "From the King." And again, "From King David." This time he whispered.

<hr />

I stood, unmoving, staring at the door for a few moments, deciding whether to open it to the news of my husband's death. Why else would he be here? But then I wondered, why would the King's guard be outside or anywhere near a place where women came to be cleansed? I must have been silent longer than my thoughts, as another urgent thump reverberated through the room. It was a public place, so I stepped out into the now dark night, lit only by moonlight and the torches the guards held aloft. I stared at the two men who stood before me as I drew my cloak tighter around me. Standing with my hands clutching my tunic, not knowing what to say, I vaguely recognised the man I now knew to be Matthew. He was a soldier, a son to my cousin. He was wounded from battle many years ago, and was now resigned to being a city foot soldier.

"My lord," I whispered. "What news do you bring?" I watched as Matthew's eyes widened, filling his face with an exhaustion I had not expected.

He bent his head slightly turning his gaze from me

"The King requires your presence at the palace." he said, his tone soft.

I was confused. Why was his countenance so wary? Why would he not even look at me? Only then did I realise that my head was uncovered and my hair unruly though I had my cloak, over my shoulders. I quickly stepped back in and dressed myself appropriately. No woman should conduct herself in such a way.

A few moments later, I was escorted into the king's chariot, waiting a few streets away. At first, I hesitated to follow beyond two streets, not sure where I was going until I glimpsed the royal cart further ahead. Only then was I reassured that I was heading to the palace. As I stepped into the empty cart, I turned to Matthew in confusion. "Where is Martha? Where is Salma?" I asked in quick succession. Salma must have been the one who told them I was here; she had left me less than an hour before.

I watched his puzzled look as I reeled more and more names – those of my friends, the wives of other soldiers in battle. Not even my father's concubine or his new wife, barely older than me, were sitting in the carriage. Surely, it could not only be my husband that was dead? Or maybe we were yet to pick them up. This was one of the bigger carriages and had room enough for at least ten more people. Only news of death or loss could be reason enough for such asummons. What if it was my husband or my father Eliam or worse, both? Would I now be a widow and an orphan?

But I heard no trumpets. The streets were empty. Nothing made sense. Confusion flowed through my body, just as freely as I imagined my blood did. I swallowed hard as I tried to rid my mouth of an unfamiliar taste. It was not anger; that taste felt like a burning. It was not even fear. I knew that taste so well. I lived with it constantly while Uriah was away. This taste was different, sour enough to make my insides curdle and saliva fill my mouth as nausea swept over me.

I tried more than once to ask Matthew why I was summoned but he did not turn to acknowledge me or even respond to my imploring questions. I chose to ignore his silence and focused on my thoughts. I knew I looked good in many ways. My head and face were fully covered, and I was dressed in a yellow tunic. It was beautiful. The fabric soft, a mixture of fine silk and something else I did not recognise. It was skilfully made by Anushka, as I looked to learn, and she let me sew the buttons and ribbons on the sleeves. I had put my hair into a weave which I could easily do myself. Unlike the bun that needed skilful hands and many brush strokes to tame it first. I had no time to put kohl on my eyes or stain my cheeks. Neither did I want to. I was going to cry. That much I knew. Panic filled my head ... and my heart. I had to remind myself to breathe. I tried to fill my thoughts with anything other than this situation as I swallowed against the unpleasant taste in my mouth. Much later that day, I discovered what the taste was. And sadly, I grew to know it so well, even more than fear. It was the taste of sorrow.

Chapter Six

The journey to the palace seemed to take longer than usual. I imagined that if I had to walk, it would take me no more than a few paces. I questioned why the two guards, led by Matthew, chose to use a route which took more time than if we had walked. Though I was not a frequent guest at the palace - I had never even been beyond the forecourt yard behind the massive gates - I passed it frequently on my way to the market where I sold my deftly woven baskets. It never took this long to arrive. I imagined a chariot would move more swiftly than my tiny legs. I started to panic.

Matthew sensed my unease and broke his silence. "We have taken the back roads. The king does not wish to make his presence known to the whole of Israel." His smile took any rancour from his words.

I hid behind my veil and also smiled at the King's foolishness. He could hide his carriage from main roads as much as he chose, but the whole City was gossiping about the fact that he was not on the battlefield. Much speculation as to why he did not go to war had spread faster than goats freed from their pen. Some said he was sick, others said he was grieving the death of one of his wives, and yet others said he was at the battle front. They believed his presence in the palace was the lie. Nobody outside of the palace walls had seen the King and nobody within the palace walls would speak as to his presence or absence.

Well, tonight, I would know for sure. I swallowed again realising the moments that waited ahead. For the first time ever, I was to meet the King face-to-face. I had seen him, of course, many times over the years, but always from a distance. I had, however, been close enough to him to see that he was a man many would describe as handsome. Though he was a respected and brilliant man of war, he was not built like a soldier. He was a head smaller in stature than most and seemed more advanced in years than many. Though I could not guess his age, I knew he was certainly older than my husband.

I had never thought about the day I would meet King David, nor did I have any desire to. I knew some things about him, having heard many stories from Uriah. Stories that made me feel like I had met the man myself. Some were filled with his courage; some with violence; and some his compassion. He loved Yahweh; that much I knew. He was unashamed in his worship of Him. When he returned from battle he would dance extravagantly in praise of his God. He was known to spend many hours in the Temple, and he made room for the prophets and priest. His constant vow was to spend his life killing all the enemies of God and he declared this boldly. So, all of Israel knew that to him, God came first.

From the day he killed the giant Goliath who dared to taunt the army of the living God, the King never backed down from any battle that would bring glory to the name of our God. Not once was it recorded that the King did not go to war until that day in early spring when I was summoned to meet him face-to-face. The day my life changed completely.

The sudden jolt of the carriage, as the horses clattered to a halt, alerted me to our arrival. I lifted my gaze to see a door that led into the palace stables. I knew that behind me to the right were the mammoth palace gates; though they seemed within reach, they were actually some distance away. The walls were illuminated with the bright lights of the many large fire pots standing high on the long fence. However, the lights where we stood were dim, casting just enough to see as I put one careful foot in front of the other.

I walked slowly behind the guards, grateful for the veil that covered not only my head but my shaking arms. My teeth chattered quietly almost in time to the thud of our footsteps on the hard floor. The hallway stretched before me so far into the distance that I could not even begin to imagine its true length. Cold and empty, the ceilings soared high above. Soft, glowing lights sent shadows dancing on golden ornaments which adorned the walls. Under different circumstances, I would have loved to take my time to stare, to touch, to smell, and to enjoy the beauty of the large oil paintings, exquisitely embroidered hangings, and tall golden vases filled with fresh flowers. My senses quivered with all there was so to see.

I had heard about the beauty of the palace, but nothing prepared me for the majesty of it all. And I had seen only a miniscule part of this vast palace. The guards stopped abruptly, as did my heart, or so I thought. Matthew tapped gently on the large oak door using a magnificent lion's head knocker made of gold with red rubies in its eyes. When there was no immediate response he knocked again — three short thuds in quick succession. This time a slave girl opened the door and peered out at us. I waited for Matthew to go in so I could follow; instead, he stepped aside, turned to me and said, "The king will see you." Then, without waiting for a response he turned around with the other soldiers, stepped aside and marched off behind me.

I was left in front of the open door. Not knowing what to do next, I let out a deep breath, not even realising I had been holding it. The slave girl stepped forward and waved her arm indicating I should enter. Hesitant, I walked forward, and she escorted me a short distance down a corridor towards another door guarded by four men. They parted ways, two stepping to the left and two to the right as we approached the door. Not one word did they utter. She then knocked three times and did not wait for a response before opening the door a few inches and motioning me through it. Before I could ask her name or even thank her, she closed the door behind me without a glance or a word. I stood there, shocked, inside a large room not knowing what I should do. Why was I here? "Yahweh," I said gently as I closed my eyes and began to pray.

Chapter Seven

As I looked around, I could see I was not alone; the King was standing at the far end of the great chamber. Though I could not see the length and breadth of it, the lights were too soft, I could tell it must be at least three times the size of my own home. Though lavish, the room was quiet and empty and the king was alone, far from the scene I had visualised. I thought at least my grandfather would be here or one of the prophets, a high priest, or even one of the King's wives.

Somebody.

Anybody.

But there was nobody — except the King, and now me.

"Come," he said, his loud voice bouncing off the large oak beams that filled the corners of the ceilings. Though I heard his command I could not move. My legs lost the ability to move as panic, mixed with fear, rendered me immobile. I tried my hardest, but I could not move. The thoughts now racing through my head were ones I did not want to even imagine.

I smelt him long before he started walking towards me. The air filled with the pungent scents of strong Arabian oils that both pleased and choked me in equal measure. As soon as he came close to me, I dropped to my knees, touching my forehead to the floor, bowing low before my King.

Again, his voice came to my ears, "Come."

I moved the only way my body allowed, I crawled on my hands and knees knowing it would be better for my life to be spared by crawling like a dog in response to the King. Not to move at all meant certain death before sunrise for disobedience.

The king quickly reached down to the ground and pulled me up. I dared not raise my gaze to meet his. I remember the slight chuckle in his voice as he mocked me. "Do your legs fail you, Bathsheba?" he asked.

I froze at his touch; he knew my name? How?

"You are beautiful, Bathsheba." He whispered in my left ear. His breathe crawled up my skin as his hands crawled up my back. He knew my name. Since he knew my name and he knew who I was, then he must also know that I am married to one of his men. He must know I am the daughter of one of his men and granddaughter of one of his closest advisors. He had to know this. So why was he touching me in such a sensual way? A way only a husband should?

When he pulled my scarf from my face, I turned so he would not see wet cheeks. But he raised my face to his and I closed my eyes so tightly I could not stare at the king.

"Fear not," he said as his thumb scraped teardrops from my cheeks. By now, I had no doubts about his intentions. He was close enough for me to feel the strength of his desire.

"Bathsheba," he whispered, his voice thick with lust, and longing. There was a familiarity in the way he called my name. It sounded like Uriah's voice, only more forcefully.

"Look at me," he commanded. So, I opened my eyes to him. He looked at me, straight at me as though assessing me; as though he was thinking or wrestling with his thoughts. Then, he turned his gaze away and released me abruptly.

Everything in me screamed for help — except my lips. No words could come out of my mouth. No matter how much I desired it. It occurred to me to try to speak to him, to beg him not to go down this perilous path, to reason with him. But it also occurred to me that I was in the presence of my King; and my life was in his hands. With one wrong word from me or one command from him, I would be dead. Just a word! But would death not be a better option? I opened my mouth but nothing came out. Loathsome weakness swept through my body setting off trembling in my limbs. I could barely walk. How could I run or scream? And even if I did, who would hear me? Who would come to my rescue? Who was strong enough or bold enough to defy the King? I sat, shivering, on the floor, helpless, hopeless, afraid, and angry. For the second time in my life, I wondered why I was born a woman. The first time had been at the death of my mother.

King David placed a goblet filled with rich red wine in my hands. The one in his own hand was empty. "Drink," he said, as he turned and walked back to a table filled with choice meats, fruits of every colour and a vast glass jug filled with the blood-red wine. I watched as he poured without measure into his large golden goblet. Drinking quickly and deeply he emptied the goblet once more before slamming it on the table and turning his back to me. The noise bounced off the rafters as it echoed through the room. I turned to look at the door, it seemed such a short distance away. I could run to it in fewer strides than it would take the king to reach me from the far side of the room where he now stood undressing.

I knew that escape was futile. There were guards on the other side of that door, armed with swords sharp enough to behead me in minutes. As though sensing my inner dilemma, the King turned to me and pointed towards the large bed that sat in the middle of the vast room. I followed his finger as though it was a voice command. He did not speak, having no need to. I was a woman, one of his subjects, and his instruction was clear. I looked towards the oversized bed. It was beautifully adorned with white and purple linen drapes hanging from the ceiling on both sides of the bed. These were pulled to the back and pinned to the walls with heavy rods.

I took in the sight of the room around me, walking as slowly as I could, no longer crawling on my knees or on my stomach like a serpent. The walls were beautiful. The one right behind the bed was adorned with gold ornaments. In the middle was a mirror which reached from floor to ceiling. I stood for a moment and stared at my reflection. My hair was still in a loose braid, my yellow dress still flowed around me, but my cheeks were red, and my eyes swollen.

When I got to the bed, I stalled for time by pushing a soft velvet cushion to one side, so I could sit only on the edge of the bed. It was one of many cushions of various shapes, colours and sizes that were scattered on the voluminous bed. My brain wondered if perhaps this was just a dream. Maybe I had misread the King's intention. Maybe in just a few moments, the doors would open and other people would walk in. But when I turned around and saw the King standing naked in front of me, I knew all my maybes were wrong.

———

I would not dare to recount in detail the events that happened next. To write them down would be a betrayal to my very soul. Those excruciating memories are tucked away deep inside me and each time they riot, I plead with Yahweh to bless me with forgiveness. In hindsight, I should have drunk the wine, just like he did. It would have numbed the pain or, at least, delayed the intense feeling of the shame that washed over me.

I cried throughout the fierce ravaging of my body. The love I shared with Uriah was tender, never painful, never rushed. With Uriah, I was never ashamed. I entered my marriage with purity vowing before God and man to honour my husband; and now, I was defiled. I knew death was imminent, either at the hands of the King or at my husband's. If he found out, he would not dare speak against his King. But I would be dragged to the marketplace, stripped and stoned to death.

When it was all over, I lay in silence wondering what would happen next. Moments later, I heard a knock on the door — three sharp busts.

"You may return to your dwelling," the king said as he donned the ruby red robe he had discarded earlier. He pushed aside voluminous white curtains which were covered in purple beads. Under normal circumstances I would have considered them beautiful. They revealed a large glass door that appeared to lead to the open air. He walked on to the roof top as, from my place on the bed, I stared at the full moon as tears poured down my face.

I dressed quickly wrapping my veil tightly around me, hoping that it not just covered my hair which was now unravelled but also my newfound shame. The same servant-girl opened the door from the outside. Matthew and two other men stood waiting. Not a word was spoken during the long walk to the chariot. The journey home seemed much quicker than the journey there. No words spoken; no glances exchanged. Just a silence that hung in the air, much louder than the darkness of night.

Chapter Eight

Much to my annoyance, Anushka awaited me at the door when I returned home. I had hoped to slip quietly into the house.

"The king's chariot, my mistress?" The inflection in her voice was a tell-tale sign of her concern.

I did not respond. I was still clutching tightly to my veil, hiding behind it as though it contained some magical protection.

"Is all well with my master?"

Her high-pitched voice tugged at the pain in my heart at the mention of Uriah. I pushed her aside and went straight to the main inner chamber. I looked at my bed, the one I shared with my husband. I loved to lay in it when he was away.

We had separate rooms, but I only used mine during the days I was unclean. I hoped to use it more when children came, but most often I shared the main bed chamber with Uriah. That was at his request. He had no other wife or concubine, and it was his desire that I stayed with him every night he was at home with the exception of my bleeding days. That night, I went into my own chamber. I knew Anushka was watching. I did not care. I could not bring myself to lay on the same bed Uriah would come home to.

Once alone, I tore off my clothes and tossed them on the floor with more vigour than I thought I could achieve. I had a strong desire to burn every single item of clothing I wore, especially my under garments. I even had the desire to burn myself. I felt dirty. I had to force myself to breathe but nothing I did stopped the tears. My head felt heavy, and I rubbed at eyes which were now prickly and raw. The last time I felt this way was when my mother was placed in a grave but even then, the tears were a mixture of sorrow and relief that mama was now free of suffering. She was with Yahweh. She was at peace.

This current pain was only filled with sorrow. There was no joy, no freedom; quite the opposite as I was now in bondage, a slave to shame. I climbed into my bed to think about how I could end my life, so I need not live with this shame. Sleep felt far away, and the smell of the King covered me like a painful rash. I threw back the bed covers and ran quickly to the bath house praying Anushka would not dare to follow me. Once there, I filled the large basin with buckets of cold water from the drum and then I scrubbed my skin until it bled, and still felt no relief. After what seemed like hours, I gave up and returned to my bed with my skin as sore as my heart. I was certain that I would not sleep that night or for many days, weeks, and months to come.

The next day I slept way past the cock's crow, it being late morning when my eyes forced themselves open. Two things shocked me. Firstly, I did not think I would or could sleep. Grief normally keeps you awake, but I soon learnt that no matter how much the mind is locked in battle, the body will over-power it when exhaustion is present. Secondly, I could barely see through the pain in my eyes.

The familiar aroma of soaked raisins filled my nostrils and pierced my numb brain, so I knew Anushka had left a hot cup of tea on the wooden table beside my bed. I reached out and grabbed it, and took a sip, grateful for the warm soothing liquid that refreshed my parched mouth. It brought unex-pected comfort. I felt a mild sense of relief from the persistent banging between my eyes. Gloom filled the room even though the sun had risen and shone brightly overhead. A thick blanket hung over the window preventing the light from entering freely. Despite this, I could still see the red marks on my arms, a reminder that the horrors of yesterday were not a dream. I shivered at the memories of the King's tight grip. The opulent rings on his fingers were surely responsible for the angry red lines that now stained my fair skin. Or were they a result of my harsh scrubbing? I put the cup down, and lay back, my head resting on the wall instead of my bed. I then released the endless tears that had filled within me overnight.

I stayed in my chambers for weeks losing count of the days; I only woke to eat, cry, and pray. Yes, pray. I found comfort in speaking to Yahweh. At first, I had set my heart against Yahweh - what kind of God would allow such wickedness to befall me without cause? And then one night, I had a dream, unlike any other dream I had ever had. My nights would often be filled with dreams. Some pleasant, some unpleasant, but each time I would awaken and completely forget them. But that night was different.

Five days after my encounter with the king. That night in my dream, I saw a flicker in my chamber as something seemed to dance with light around me - a firefly. It was the only light in the thick darkness of the night. I reached out my hand to catch it, fascinated by its beauty and each time it flew out of my reach. So, I followed it, determined to catch it, but it kept dancing just out of reach, seeming to play a game with me: flitting close then darting away. Laughter bubbled up inside me and flew from my lips. When the firefly flew outside the window I followed it, running around the field just outside my dwelling, underneath a star-filled sky.

It was there, in the field, that I saw a swarm of fireflies, larger than any I had ever seen in my life. As I looked up at them, they suddenly moved towards me and wrapped around me, lifting me off my feet with a tender embrace. They tickled my skin; they kissed my lips; they danced on my eyelids; they even stroked my hair. They filled me with such joy as they moved all around me. Then I heard a gentle whisper, as though from the belly of the swarm, *"My beloved Bathsheba, let your hope not depart from Me, I have you in the palm of My hands. Be at peace, My child."*

I awoke with a start, jumped out of my bed, searching frantically around me, as I tried to pull myself together. I was drenched in my own sweat.

My heart beat loudly threatening to pound its way from my body. I forced myself to breathe as I screamed, "Yahweh!" I fell to my knees to worship my Lord. From that night prayers became my comfort. I spent my days clinging to the memories and peace that overwhelmed me as I put my hope back into the Lord my God.

Anushka asked me every day to speak with her, but I could not. What was I to say? How could I explain what happened? My silence protected me; or so I thought. Each day Anushka told me everything that was happening around me: the fights in the marketplace, the traders who were previously thought lost at sea who returned with much praise to God, the reports from great progress at the war, and many more interesting titbits of news. She left nothing out, especially the sudden death of Matthew, two of the King's foot soldiers, one of the Kings' concubines and two slaves.

Chapter Nine

That night after hearing of those sudden deaths, I could not sleep as the hand of fear gripped me. Was I next? It seemed that the ones who had fallen were the ones who were present that night. Was it a coincidence, or was the King so determined to cover his actions at the expense of the lives of those called to serve him? Anger filled me to my core, threatening to overpower me as there was no room for expression. Bitterness filled my mouth at the fact that now, only the King and I knew what happened that night. It felt like both a blessing and a curse. Uriah was not expected home for months to come according to the reports from the war. For once, I was grateful for his absence. Perhaps in these next months, my heart would regain its composure and the Lord would spare me the shame and wipe it from my memory. My plea to the Lord that the secret would remain buried along with the memories.

Yet, in my heart I knew that I could not lie to Uriah, he was a good man. Forsaking his own land and coming to live in and fight for another, he was committed to the King. The betrayal would cut too deep, it would wound him deeply knowing that the man he went to war for had brought the battle to his own home. And then I thought about my father Eliam, also at war for the King, and my grandfather Ahitophel at service in the King's palace.

"Oh King David, why did you do such a thing?" My heart grieved over again as my anxious heart darted towards the only solution — death. In my heart I knew I had two choices — silence or sacrifice. I could live with the secret and pretend nothing happened; no one knew except the King. Or I could take my own life to preserve the secret and honour the King and my husband.

I considered running away instead, leaving Jerusalem, and going to a country on the other side of the Jordan. Perhaps I would be sold into slavery or find work in a temple. My beauty went ahead of me; I would have no trouble finding a master. But the more I thought about running, the more I realised how foolish an idea it was. Should I leave Jerusalem, a daughter of Yahweh, to go and serve in a temple? Would it not be better to remain at home and stay silent than end up a slave? I nodded my head in agreement with myself: there was only one real option — death. It was the safest option. To my own heart I had to be true. I could not lie to my husband to save my own life; I would not even be able to give my body to him to touch without anguish. How could his lips meet mine bringing joy when I still tasted the kiss of the King's betrayal on my very soul?

In the morning, my mind was made up. I was going to go through the fields and beyond the Kidron Valley to the deep side of the Gihon where the water current was high and fierce, and the river was deep. There, I would lay in the arms of

Yahweh till He brought me home. I wondered what sacrifice I would take with me; perhaps two young pigeons; they would be easiest to carry in a satchel without question. I looked in my basket for some coins and was reminded that I had not been to the market to sell my wares for weeks. It was a blessing that Uriah always left more than enough to care for my needs. My trade was not only for profit, but also for talking amongst the women to release myself from loneliness and idleness. Both, I had revelled in these last few weeks.

As I gathered myself quietly so as not to rouse Anushka, I heard her footsteps behind me and then a pause and a sigh. Could she read my mind? It was my love for her that prompted my silence. No one else could know, even as I prepared to go to my own grave. So why did I feel guilty for shutting her out?

I turned slowly to meet her eyes, perhaps for the last time. I wanted to pull her into a warm embrace and thank her for loving me, for caring for me, for being patient with me. I wanted to plead with her to look after Uriah and serve him and her next mistress with the same dedication and compassion as she served me. I considered releasing her from slavery, but who would tend Uriah's home in his absence? Would he return home months later to an empty, unclean house? I was so lost and preoccupied in my own thoughts and anguish that it took me a few minutes to realise what was in Anushka's hands. My gaze moved quickly from her wet eyes to her now empty hands as the unsoiled cloths fell at her feet, still white, clean, and unused.

Chapter Ten

My hands flew to my stomach. It dawned on me that my time had passed, and my uncleanness had not shown. I relieved myself of last night's raisin cake and lamb and then staggered to the bed to sit.

Fresh water was poured on my face, and I felt my legs lifted as I lay back on the bed. "Rest, my lady," said Anushka. The firmness in her voice brooked no argument. Shock stemmed the tears that should have poured from down my face. I watched, eyes wide open, as Anushka cleaned the floor without uttering a word before leaving my chambers. Grateful for her absence I allowed myself think — could I be pregnant?

Maybe an hour later, maybe longer, I heard Anushka come into my chambers. She opened the window slightly to let both light and air come in. I must have fallen asleep without even knowing. I realised I could not take my own life. It was no longer just mine and I had to speak; I needed to tell her the truth. The smell of the tea I loved so much suddenly turned my stomach and I pushed away the cup as it neared me. My whole world felt like it was falling apart. Within me, a battle ravaged my soul as raw emotions threatened to consume me. Sorrow and joy simultaneously stole my peace. Motherhood, a mystery I craved to unravel was upon me, but not for the one with whom I had prayed for. I was pregnant from the king's seed.

Anushka sat on the floor beside my bed. I knew she was waiting for me to speak. To explain. I also knew that she was extending me a courtesy based on our mutual affection because she had every right to bring this matter before the elders and have me stoned in the marketplace. What other explanation could there be for a woman whose husband had been at war for months to be with child except that she had played the harlot?

I felt her hand warm on my skin, calling my attention to her.

"Trust me with the truth, my lady," she urged. I closed my eyes and felt the liquid drip down my face and try to seep through my clenched lips. The memories, which had not stayed buried, rushed through my veins like ice cold water. The hair on my skin stood erect at these thoughts. Where do I begin? How do I even start to recount the tale of what befell me? I had no words; I had spoken only few except in prayer. Did God even hear me? If He did, why would this great affliction come upon me?

"Whose child fills your womb, my lady. Please tell me what you have done." Her shaky voice filled the room as she gave way to her own sorrow.

Her words infuriated me. What have *I* done? Me? What did *I* do? I was not responsible for this. Countless times I had blamed myself. I could have done more. I should have fought harder. I should have refused and accepted death instead. Then, countless times I reminded myself that I stood in the presence of a man that even my own husband and my own father would lie face down before. How could I have dared to open my mouth to the King?

I hated the way I felt in that moment - vulnerable, insignificant, and helpless. I lived in a world where I could be put to death by my own husband without recourse, a world where, as a woman, I had no rights, no choice, no voice. And yet, here I was and the question that lingered in the air unanswered reminded me that it was I who had a shame to carry; it was I who was burdened with an explanation to give; one that could mean my life or my death depending on whose ears it fell upon. I was the one who needed to answer to what I had done.

Without thinking, I touched the scar that now remained underneath my left arm: it served as a constant reminder; it was small, still red against my skin but no longer painful unlike the larger one on the inside of my right thigh. On the King's right hand, he wore a large ring on his third finger. It was made of gold and onyx and had horns. One of these cut a deep gouge in my thigh. On his left he wore two smaller rings: one was raised with three red stones and the other smooth. It was the first that cut my inner arm as he lifted it without regard. Deafened by either wine or passion, he did not even hear me scream in pain.

Again, she tapped me.

This time, I looked at Anushka, "The king." That was all I could say in the moment. That was all I needed to say.

I saw her body start to shake, mirroring mine, and then she put her head between her thighs and wept. We stayed like that for several hours — steeped in collective grief.

At noon she got up and went to bring food. Before she left, she placed her hands on my cheeks, looked straight into my eyes, and said, "This burden you carried alone these last weeks is now mine to share, you have my loyalty and my trust." She kissed me on my forehead and left without saying another word.

I sat in regretful silence, wishing I had spoken sooner. The type of grief I carried would have been lighter with the counsel of a friend. Silence was heavy and painful.

Chapter Eleven

Anushka's footsteps were now a much welcome relief. I smiled as she set a plate before me, a mixture of dry bread, fresh fruit, fish, and tea with mint leaves. "You must eat, if not for yourself but for the baby you carry." She held the mint leaves close to me and the scent was both welcome and soothing. I drank it, burning my tongue in my haste. I only managed a few morsels of bread and a handful of grapes. I felt a need to be outside, in a way that I had not longed for in weeks. It surprised me. Now was the time I should hide even more, yet now was the time I wanted to go out: as though a rebellion beckoned, and I wanted to respond. "Let us go down by the fields," I said, standing up to get dressed.

Anushka pulled me down. "No, my lady! Will you not pass the houses of many along the road, some of whom are your friends and who would expect that you should be unclean?"

I heard her wisdom; this was not the time for me to be out and about. Living in a small community with the women of soldiers, we knew each other's moon cycles because we met each other at the Mikveh when it was time to be cleansed. It was also there that we saw who was not present and knew who had been taken with child.

I pushed the curtains aside, removed the blanket that had brought deep darkness and then opened the window so wide that I could climb out of it if I dared. It was the closest I would get to being outside for the next few days. I was lucky that I lived in a house with my own chambers and so I did not have to go to the communal tent like the women who did not have this small luxury. There were many women who had to spend their unclean days separated from their household. I stood up and paced the length and breadth of my room rubbing my stomach. I started to pray, thanking Yahweh for the gift of a child and pleading for mercy. Even if I was to die for this sin, I prayed that He would let the child live for His glory. It baffled me that for many years I had lain with my husband and had nothing to show for it, but just one night with the King and I was with child. I was overcome by the spirit of motherhood. Only hours ago, I was willing to give up my life for myself and now I was willing to keep my life to save the one I carried within.

As Anushka cleared the dishes and left the chambers, I went to the corner of the small room to pray; this was the same spot where I had first seen the firefly in my dream weeks ago. I thought, perhaps God was there.

"Yahweh, my God. The one who said, *'Let not your hope depart from me,'* help me. Even now, more than ever, I need your help. Hide me, protect me. These nine months, keep my husband at war, so that I may bear this son within me and maybe even nurse him a week or two before my life is taken from me. Grant that my son shall live before I die." More words spilled out of me. Some I remember, some I don't, but my heart's cry was plain. I was desperate for my son to live. I don't know how I knew it, but I knew — it was a boy within me.

I held tight to my abdomen as though protecting the infant with human hands. By now, I lay on the cold floor with only my scarf as a blanket. I heard the words from deep within my soul as though they were whispered in my ears. *"Send word to the King."* Startled, I turned my face to the door; I was alone. Anushka had not returned. What was Yahweh asking of me? To tell the King I carried his child? What good would come of that?

I did my best to ignore the quiet voice that spoke; there was so much more to think about and to plan. Things like how I would go to the priest monthly with my offering and then to the Mikveh to ensure I was still being seen but would not enter the bath to cleanse. That way, my friends and others would see me and assume that all was well with me while my husband was away. I had heard a few people came to check in on me. To one Anushka had insisted that I had a fever. To another she said I had journeyed to visit with my father's family. Another time, she said I was with my grandfather who had taken ill with a fever. Each time, the story was unquestioned for no one had reason to think otherwise. The stories were well received.Yet, telling the King could change things.

Fear tasted bitter in my mouth. "No, Yah..." I started to say but stopped myself before I blasphemed the name of the Lord. Should I fear the King more than I feared God? If I could not refuse the King, what right did I have to speak against the God of Israel who had commanded me to send word to the King?

"Yes, Lord. I will do as you command."

I sighed, my heart heavy, but moved my feet towards obedience. I stepped into the living quarters for the first time in many weeks and took everything in as though seeing it for the first time. The house was modest, made with wood, bricks and mud. There were some tasteful furnishings from various parts of the kingdom. Some were bought, others brought as spoils of war. There were wooden chairs covered with hand-sewn cushions that I stuffed with lambs' wool. A water jug, that was filled by Anushka most days with fresh water from the river, stood tall in the corner by the door. It was a beautiful ornament, made by a philistine slave and bought as a gift from Uriah. Something about that jug made water taste cooler and sweeter. Perhaps because the clay used to craft it was thickened twice over or maybe it was the taste of a love gift.

There was also a lamp that I loved. The gentle glow from its wood-filled light made any evening feel special. I had missed sitting on the chair beside it, with pillows under my feet as I heard Anushka sing; or as I listened to Uriah tell stories. From the corner of my eyes, I could see the door that led to Uriah's room on the other side of the living quarters. I hastily turned my gaze away. Instead, I looked towards the outhouse where I thought Anushka would have gone. It was then that I saw the stained rug at the far corner, leaning against a wall; and I felt a wave of sadness. I remembered the last night I shared with Uriah, sitting outside in front of our home. We placed the rug underneath the stars on the small patch of grass near the rosebush that gave a sweet fragrance especially at night.

I longed for moments like that again, wondering if they would ever come yet, knowing it was now an impossible dream. In a single night, with one swift act of lust, the King had ruined the life I had.

I waited impatiently for Anushka to return from the outhouse. She enjoyed a cool bath in the middle of the day when the sun was hottest. I preferred a bath at night as it made for a better sleep. I sat in the living quarters alone, humming quietly. I did not want to pray. I thought perhaps the Lord would tell me something more difficult to do and I exercised mild rebellion.

My mother always told me to fear Yahweh. One of the last things she said to me was: "Obey His voice, Bathsheba." Also, "Listen to His words, Bathsheba."

I heard her voice in my mind as clear as it was all those years ago. Sometimes, I wish I did not believe, but I was never one to understand the point of serving a carved wooden God. How people could make something with their own hands and then worship it bewildered me. It was one of the minor differences I had with Anushka: she carried her little wooden gods with her almost all the time. I wondered if she ever heard them speak the way Yahweh speaks to me.

When she finally arrived and saw me sitting in the living quarters, her smile showed it was a welcome surprise. But when the words came out of my mouth her brow creased as she tossed her long, wet, black hair.

She collapsed on the floor, her tiny frame making little sound. "Does your God wish you stoned to death?" she asked, pointing at me. Removing one of her Egyptian gods from her pocket she shoved it in my face as though trying to imply her goddess would never suggest such a thing. I chuckled: this same goddess had a temple filled with young women sold into harlotry. Her gods, who required human sacrifices, were powerless in the face of Yahweh. I would rather die for the sake of my God if that was His will.

I had heard many stories about my God, from the parting of the Red Sea, to manna from heaven, and so much more. But my hope was not even based on what I had been told about Yahweh, but what I had heard and experienced myself. Even as a child, I had had encounters with Yahweh and even now, though it seemed like a death sentence awaited me, I had an unusual peace. "Whether death awaits me or not, I must send word to the King, and you will take it to him," I said to her, and watched as her eyes widened in disbelief.

"Me? How? What right do I have to request audience with the king? I am not even one of you, I am an Egyptian slave."

I laughed at her outburst as I saw panic grip her and fear flit across her face.

Chapter Twelve

I shifted, making room for her to join me so I could speak more gently. The walls have ears sometimes. "No, not your lips to the king, but your lips to your lover. I want you to help me summon him and he will tell the King." I teased her gently. "You think I don't know you have my Saba's affection? My grandfather was never one to turn his eye from such beauty." I said, holding my hand under her chin as she blushed.

"Would that not cause distress to your grandfather? Can he hold such a matter to heart without asking many questions of the King? And your father? Would word not reach him about your predicament and then to the ears of my lord Uriah? Let me instead send word through the food bearer. We have much in common and are well acquainted. I can trust her with this word. As she lays the meal before the King, she will lay the news at his feet."

I took only a moment to see her reasoning. She was right. My grandfather would be filled with fury, and I could not predict how he would react. Honour bound to the King and to our ways, perhaps he may even have dragged me himself to be stoned, not caring to protect the child. I grabbed Anushka's hand, squeezed it, and said, "Do as you see fit, but please let the morning not come before you have sent word to the King."

She nodded. As she stood up to leave, she paused and asked, "Tell me, my mistress. What happened that night?"

My eyes filled with tears I did not know still lingered as the memories once more flooded my brain. I recounted the tale leaving no detail unspoken, from the minute I entered the chariot, to the King's bed chamber and back to my home defiled. I shared it all, even showing the scars from the King's rings I had hidden till that moment. I felt her warm embrace which reminded me of my mother. I wept more. I wished she was alive. She always knew what to do and say, a woman so wise beyond words. I missed her.

"You are not to blame; this was not your doing. Can any woman be saved from the passionate lust of a man? Worse if that man is the king. Your wishes mean nothing." The truth of her words brought both comfort and anger. Can a woman truly be saved from the lust of a man?

Removing myself from her embrace, I felt her heavy heart. She arose, and without much hesitation, strapped on her sandals and left.

When she returned that evening, all Anushka said was, "The word has reached his ears."

I waited for more, not sure what to expect, or if I would get a response, but I had done what I had been instructed by Yahweh to do. She said nothing more but started to prepare a meal for us to share.

I too stayed silent and found myself praying once more.

"Yahweh, I have done as you have asked. My life and my son are in Your hands." I repeated this fervent prayer over and over waiting to hear more from the Lord, but His silence was louder than His command.

Three days came and went, until one day as I sat by the window in my bed chamber, Anushka entered. I took one look at her face and my stomach started to churn. I thumped my chest in order to attempt relief from the pain that now clogged it. "My lord Uriah's horse has been seen at the gate; it appears he was summoned by the king." The minute the words left her mouth blackness overcame me and I slumped from my chair to the floor.

I gasped for air as something cold and wet hit my face. Water. As I rubbed my face, I stared at Anushka hoping this was a dream. I screamed, "Seen by whom? Are you sure it was his horse? How do you know it was his horse? All the horses look the same; some horses are killed and replaced; just because you saw a horse does not mean it was his and how do you even know he was summoned?" The questions tumbled out as I did not even pause for breath.

"The horse was seen by me." She responded. "I know it is my lord's horse for it bears the cloth you braided with red twine and purple silk on its right hoof."

I sat up and shook my head as though it would erase the truth. It was his horse. I had made him that cloth as a gift; it was cut from a silk garment my father gave to me on the night of my wedding. It had belonged to my mother, was both precious and expensive, and had been brought by merchants all the way from Corinth.

The first time Uriah was due to go to war after our marriage period, I had sewn it for him. Sick with love, I wanted him to take a piece of me to war with him. Aside from the gifts of gold jewellery, the most expensive thing I owned and loved was my purple garment. I cut a piece and strengthened it with earthen red twine, wrapping it around in a circle so that he could wear it on his arm, his neck or wherever he chose. He told me then that he would wear it on his horse, that life or death in battle most times relied on the speed and strength of the horse and so if any luck or blessing was contained in the cloth, it was best suited on the one who carried him thence and returned him home. Ever since, every horse he had ever ridden bore that cloth, there was no mistaking what Anushka had seen, Uriah was back.

Chapter Thirteen

Hearing footsteps at the door we both froze, but a gentle knock suggested it was more a guest than a home-owner. Anushka rushed to the door to greet Salma who had in her hand ritual cleansing cloths, oil, and two pigeons in a basket. The sun was setting and as she made her way to the tent and then the Mikveh, she called on me for company. Having not seen me for many weeks, she still knew our monthly bleeding shared a common pattern. I asked Anushka to welcome her in to wait in the living quarters while I got dressed, wondering whether to go or not. I could tell her that my flow extended a day more which was not unusual. The moon could cause the pattern to shift, and the length of days was not always predictable. But if I went with her, it would quieten any suspicions of my absence these last few weeks.

I paced the room until Anushka entered and urged me to take my ritual things and go with Salma. She said she would take the time to go to the palace gates and see if she could find out more.

As I walked with Salma, I allowed her to do all the talking. I must have missed half of what she said as my mind bounced with unanswered questions. How was I supposed to face my husband tonight? His matter with the King would be settled and he would return home to not only a defiled wife, but a pregnant one. I was so preoccupied that I did not hear Salma, but I felt the sharp twinge from her tiny palm as it hit my neck almost causing me to drop my basket as my veil fell from my face.

"Are you not rejoicing at the news of Moriah," she squealed.

"What happened to her," I asked rubbing my neck, wondering how such a small fist could hurt so much.

"She is with child, two months have come and gone," she said, her voice shrill with joy for her older sister. "Rest your mind, Bathsheba. Each time we come to Mikveh, your face is swollen with grief. Our season will come when our stomachs will be filled. These husbands we have at war help little, but Yahweh will bless us. Until then, we should rejoice with others." She pulled my arm to quicken our steps.

I looked beyond to see the palace gates as we passed the road that led to the City of David. Dread and longing filled my bones in equal measure, but what filled my mouth was the sour taste of fear. I was certain that reckoning would come to my house before the night was over.

When my turn came to present my pigeons to the priest, I was unsure what curse I would place on myself by offering a ritual when none was required. Shortly after I was to be stepping into the ritual cleansing bath when I had no need, afraid I had already brought a curse upon my head, I chose not to enter the bath; instead, I walked to the corner of the room opposite where the large bath rested, close to where the fresh stream was connected from which the cleansing water was rumoured to flow from Gihon.

There was another window in the room, one I had never taken much notice of, as beyond it was a wall made of mud and wooden slabs. I am not sure why I was suddenly drawn to it, but I walked closer and looked out as the sun still gave light. I looked up ahead of me, only then realising I could see the roof of the palace in the distance. I stood, mouth open, recognising that if I could see the roof, anyone on that roof could also see me. I stepped back and saw the distance between the bath and the window was mere feet in the small room. It was then I realised that though a wall existed beyond the window to provide privacy for the women who came to cleanse, there was no protection above the wall. From the roof of the palace, the tallest building in all of Jerusalem, a woman could be seen. That was how the King first saw me; that was how the soldiers knew where to find me.

Instinctively, I wrapped my arms around my body, as though I could cover what had been uncovered many weeks ago. Stumbling back from the window, it started to make sense to me now. I had many sleepless nights wondering how the King even knew I existed and why he called for me. Clarity brought no relief; knowing how and why changed nothing except that I decided to sew a thick curtain for the window. I would call it a gift to the holy temple if asked by Miriam, the widow whose job it was to open the bathing area, clean it, and close the doors at the end of the day.

By the time I emerged, Salma was dressed and waiting. We walked back towards our quarters; now clean, we could mingle with our community again and we even stopped to buy fresh fruit, freely touching them to sample the platters on display. I placed two large pomegranates in my basket, although I enjoyed grapes and dried figs most, Uriah loved the red juice of the pomegranate. Salma's dwelling was many houses before mine, so I left her with good wishes and walked much more slowly towards home. Surely, Uriah would have come by now. The sun was setting fast and warriors who returned from battle were usually sent home quickly for a meal and comfort.

Anushka sat alone as I pushed the door open, rising quickly to greet me. I was surprised that he was not home but eager for news from the palace. "Uriah is no longer with the King; he remains at the gate with the king's servants. I have seen him with my own eyes. He has laid a mat on the floor and sits there quietly. Beside him was a woven basket of fine linen with gifts from the King"

Her words stung my ears and the pain they caused was so much more than anything I had ever encountered. I did not understand; none of this made any sense. He promised me that he would always come home. He asked me never to come running at the sound of the trumpets, that instead, I should wait, and he would come. Tonight, he did not come home, instead he choose to be with the king's servants.

"Perhaps he considers your monthly flow and thinks you are unclean." Anushka offered her words to try and bring comfort, but being unclean did not mean being ignored or abandoned? Just because he could not touch me, did not mean he could not see me.

"No, Anushka, the king has surely given him word." I snapped, confused.

"Let the night pass. Dawn will meet me at the door of the palace, and I will bring word from the food bearer, my lady." She said, patting my arm gently.

I stepped into my inner chamber with a heavy heart. It was one thing for him to be so far away fighting God's enemies, that distance I understood and could bear, but it was another thing for him to be so close, almost within my touch and yet so far away. My emotions rushed in and out of reason, even if he did come home, then what? What exactly would I say or do?

That night was long. Sleep evaded me so I embraced prayer instead. Speaking to Yahweh brought me comfort, even though He remained silent. This time though I did not mind; I was the one who had so much to say. I poured out my heart, my fears, my wishes, and my hopes. After all, He told me to hope in Him, so I did.

It was not yet dawn when I heard Anushka slam the front door. I immediately rose and got ready to go to the palace gate. I put on Anushka's red garment, though it hung loose around the hips and trailed on the floor. I did not mind. For what I intended to do that morning meant I had to remain unrecognised. Grabbing a black scarf I tied it firmly around my head, covering my hair and my face, leaving only a slit for me to see. I hurried to the gate, holding two empty baskets, covered with another scarf. I did not want to appear like I wandered the street without purpose, so the baskets suggested I was either trading or buying. I picked up my pace as I neared the gates.

There were many people entering and leaving through the palace gates: some, slaves at work; others, merchants; but mostly tourists who came to see the majesty of the palace in Jerusalem, famous around the nations. There were temple guards from the house of the Lord, sitting near the gates with a handful of soldiers enjoying a breakfast of wheat, figs and honey. The noise as they ate told me this. As I approached the forecourt, I immediately recognised him. There sat my husband, Uriah. His back was to me, but I would recognise him even in the dark. He was in the company of another set of soldiers, and they laughed at something he said but I did not hear.

I walked all the way around the four pillars that stood in the centre court; it had a tall water fountain filled with coins. It was here that the tourists and even my people came to toss in a silver or gold coin as some said prayers to Yahweh, some to false gods. The fountain was often emptied, and the coins added to the treasury of the King. I hid behind a tall oak tree, now having full sight of my husband. I was close enough to see him, close enough to hear his voice. I stared at him for hours, watching him closely. I wanted to reach out to him, to touch him, to speak to him. He seemed at peace; it was unlikely that the king had told him I was with child.

I did not realise how long I had been standing there until I heard my stomach rumble and a wave of nausea reminded me that my stomach craved dry bread. For the last few days, the mornings had been difficult. I often felt sick usually waking up to empty my stomach of the dinner from the night before. But some mint tea and dry bread seemed to settle me. The sun was wide awake by this time as people scurried around searching for shade. I picked up my baskets and as I prepared to make my way home, I took one more look and lingered a few moments more. At that moment, Uriah got on his feet; he rubbed his big palms together and then dusted dry grains off his chest. He turned towards the oak tree and I felt his gaze upon me. It was only for a moment that he paused, and then he stretched his tall body, picked up his mat and walked away, towards the doors of the servant quarters.

Chapter Fourteen

The journey back home was bitter. I stopped more than once to empty my stomach. I doubted it was the child inside me that made me sick. My heart was shattered. I loosened the scarf from around my face, giving me space to breathe. I saw Anushka outside the front door waiting to receive me and hurried towards her, desperate for news.

"Where have you been, my lady? I was afraid something had happened to you." She opened the door. We walked in, and she closed it firmly behind us. "Why are you dressed in this manner?" she asked.

"I went to the palace gate, I had to see for myself." A deep sigh escaped my lips. There was no need to lie. I sounded pathetic, I knew it, but I needed to see him. The taste of betrayal filled my mouth once more and then shame washed over me. I held my stomach and rubbed it gently, everything I did, and would always do, was to protect this child. I only wanted him to live, even if I died.

Anushka shifted from one foot to the other, forcing my attention towards her. "The food bearer tells me that Uriah was only summoned to give account of the war with Rabbah at Ammon. He brings good news of progress. The King did instruct him to go to his house and wash his feet, nothing more was said aside matters of war."

We both exchanged confused looks. It made no sense. "So why did Uriah not come home?" I said, thinking aloud.

She paused as though in the same thought as I, then said, "Let us wait and see what the day brings, he may come home soon."

I bid Anushka well and flew, trembling, to my inner chamber, taking my jumbled thoughts with me. I did not bother to ask who she heard the news from, friend or lover. It did not matter, what I fought to understand was why? Unless the king had already summoned Uriah before the news of my pregnancy reached him and we were faced with coincidence, yet even that seemed unlikely.

I laid down to rest but was disturbed by Anushka who bore a tray of food. The smell of mint tea tickled my nostrils and I sat up to eat. The day was far gone, and I relished the meal, eating everything set before me. I was sipping the last of my tea when Anushka rose to her feet suddenly placing her hand on her head as though she had the need to hold it down firmly.

"Ah, my lady, now I see the wisdom of the king."

I placed the cup down beside me, pushing the empty tray away. "What do you mean?" My interest piqued.

"Pardon me, my lady. I hope not to speak out of turn, but perhaps the king summoned my lord to come home from war on purpose knowing that any soldier who returned from battle of length will find pleasure in a warm meal and in the bed of his wife. If my master comes and lays with you tonight, then...."

I put my hands over her mouth to silence her. I did not need her to complete her words; I knew exactly what she was going to say.

I needed to bathe. I thought the pleasure of cool water flowing on my body might bring me some sort of relief as my body burned as I pondered Anushka's words. What manner of deception is this? How can I conceive for one man and place the responsibility on another? My spirit felt unsettled within me. What if Uriah did come home, can I go along with this? It appeared there was no length the King was unwilling to go to cover his choice. *His choice.* One for which I now had to bear the consequences and live with the guilt of raising a prince as a servant of the King.

At this point I saw no other option; it would preserve the life of my son and it would preserve mine. The child I bore was innocent and deserved a chance to live, regardless of the cost. I called for Anushka to prepare for me a bath with scented oils. She scrubbed my skin, then soaked a piece of white cloth in hot rose oil and rubbed my skin until it not only smelled of heaven but glowed and was supple to the touch. Then she braided my hair loosely, just the way Uriah liked it, so it was easy for him to untangle. I dressed in a new tunic — a bright red gown that was hand-stitched days ago by Anushka. She had taken the wooden lamp and sat outside in the cool evening breeze to stitch the fabric into a long dress. She carefully sewed in beads of many colours around the neck causing it to shimmer. She had started stitching the dress weeks ago and was determined to finish it that night. It seemed like a good way to pass time and I too picked up basket reeds and started to weave. We both sat in silence and worked for hours into the night.

As I prepared to welcome my husband, my heart began to welcome the idea. Not because I was not grieved, but because I suddenly saw a way out, a way to bring my child to life, a way to protect the child and protect me, to cover my shame and hopefully redeem the guilt I carried. I would not have chosen this path, no woman would, but life does not always follow the pattern we plan or expect. Maybe, this was Yahweh's way of protecting me. I wondered, was His hand in this? After all He told me to send word to the King, but the more I thought about it, the more I doubted it. Would a righteous God do this?

While my eyes were being darkened with kohl, I closed them tightly and prayed, "Yahweh, help me. Forgive me for this sin as I prepare for my husband's return." It was one thing to betray my husband and another to betray my God.

My heart was heavy, fear filled it like the bricks that were laid beneath my feet as a foundation. I did not know what I was going to do when Uriah walked in. I tried not to think about it. Fully dressed and ready, I walked into my husband's bed chamber. I had not been in there for weeks. Everything was untouched, just the way I had left it a month ago. I reprimanded myself for leaving the room unattended and busied myself dusting the wooden stool, the lamp, the lambskin rug and shaking out the bed linen. I unfolded the blanket, set back the curtains and then opened the window to let the evening breeze in. I then went outside to fetch the iron jar with scented oil, put a fire to light it and allowed it fragrance the room.

I sat and waited!

Chapter Fifteen

Many hours passed and the sun was falling asleep; still Uriah did not come home. I swept at my face feeling uneasy, well foolish, as my palms turned black from the kohl running down my face. Anushka sat outside the door singing a new song. When she saw me, she got up and put on her sandals. "I will go to the palace and see what is keeping him," she said, leaving me where I was standing.

With every atom of my body, I wanted Uriah home. If indeed he came to me, I would be alive to raise this child and, now that Yahweh had opened my womb, I was sure more children from my own husband would follow. Surely, Yahweh had to bless this sacrifice I was making to honour the King and to give life to the one He had given to me as a gift. "Yahweh, please bring Uriah home to me." I prayed louder, just in case He had not heard the first time.

The silence of the Lord was broken finally but the words He spoke brought me no clarity. *"Sleep now my child, be at peace."*

Sleep? Sleep alone? I did not want to sleep alone. I was waiting to sleep with my husband.

Moments later, I heard footsteps at my door; I rushed into the arms of Anushka. Her countenance invoked sorrow for her eyes were downcast. She then told me words that still linger in my ears today, words that at the time did more than steal hope from my soul; it tore me open and left me bare.

"I have just received word from the food bearer. She set a meal before the King and was present when Uriah was summoned. When the King asked him why he had not set foot at his home after a long journey, my lord replied that he will do no such thing. He said while the Ark of Israel and the servants of the Lord are out in tents in the open fields, he will not go to his house to eat and drink nor lie with his wife. He swore with his life that as long as the king lives, he will do no such thing."

My ears burned and my stomach turned at the news.

I spat on the floor repulsed. My fate had been sealed - Uriah was not coming home. His loyalty to the Crown was at once his honour and my undoing. It was this faithfulness to his service that earned him his esteemed position. I remembered the night my father summoned me and told me who he had chosen for me as my husband. He spoke about Uriah with so much pride; he had chosen for me a man who loved God and Israel more than he loved his life; and such a man would guard me with his life. Such a man, in his eyes, was worthy of his precious daughter. And now, I can see what my father saw in him — the faithful soldier, a man willing to give up his own life and deny his own pleasure for the sake of his King. If only he knew that the king he honoured so much had defiled his wife; that the King he fought for despised him and had ridiculed him.

It angered me that my husband spurned the comfort of his own home thinking it less than his duty to the King, even when commanded by the King to return home. Held back by his own will, Uriah chose not to come home to me. He broke his promise; he said he would always come to me. Did he not think I would hear from others that he was at the palace gates? Did it not matter to him that I longed for him?

I wished at that moment I had run to him and told him the truth, just to hurt him as much as his absence hurt me. I did not care, even if it had cost me my life. But for the child I carried, I probably would. Israel needed to know exactly what the man they called "king" was like. I spat on the floor again in an attempt to rid myself of the bitter taste of hatred that filled my mouth and ran through my veins.

The word of the Lord came to me again.

"*Sleep my child, be at peace.*"

I turned towards the window where darkness lurked. I fixed my eyes on it searching for peace. Where was this peace of which my Lord spoke? Only then, in the middle of the dark clouds, did I see a solitary star twinkling at me. It was then I saw the light of the Lord's presence. I looked at the bed, the one I had shaken and set with new linen hours ago, climbed into it and slept.

The next morning, I did not rise at dawn like I had the previous day. Instead, I lingered in bed and enjoyed the comfort. This bed was much softer than mine, it was also larger. I decided to rest a while longer, so I ignored the tap on the door. This room Anushka would not enter freely. I turned to face the wall. My mind wandered back to the day before as I relived the memory of my husband's presence in the city. I called forth his face, remembering every line, his strong jaw as it moved from side to side when he laughed. His laughter was loud as though it erupted from his soul. Uriah was tall, almost two heads above me and built like a man of war. It seemed like the strength in his arms was enough to lift a whole cow. He certainly lifted me without effort and enjoyed tossing me from one arm to the other.

I loved the way he left his hair cut low to his head, although yesterday it had grown in only a few months to cover his eyes. His skin the colour of wet sand glowed without oil, probably from many hours in the sun. The more I thought of him, the more sorrow filled me. I was tired of crying. By this time, I realised it changed nothing. Yes, it brought relief, but it also brought pain in my head and eyes. I wiped the unwelcome tear that slipped out without permission. "No more tears," I told myself.

When Anushka knocked again, I decided to rise and feed my unborn child. It was merely weeks and yet I could sense the life growing in my womb, or so I allowed myself to believe. Since Uriah was not coming home, I did not know what the future held for me and my unborn son, but I decided to spend the rest of my time praying for him and talking to him. I would not spend my days feeling sorry for myself. There was nothing I could do now to change the past. Neither did I control my future. My only choice was to find a way to be at peace.

Chapter Sixteen

Though it was early in the morning I had a longing for cooked lamb stew. I sat with Anushka as she prepared the meal in the kitchen. Although I invited her many times to share my meal with me, she always refused and held on to the custom, choosing to eat only after I had long finished mine. I waited in the kitchen for her as I had decided to walk into the market square — my stall had been abandoned for weeks now — and I had little desire to start trading again. There was little need as the coin purse was still full and the wives of the King's men were often sent gifts of food, watered wine, and sometimes, fine fabric and jewellery. I lacked nothing.

As we strolled, I shared some stories I had heard from my mother, thinking before my baby arrived, I could practise with Anushka. It occurred to me that for most of my life I had been a story-hearer and never a storyteller. I was deep in story-land when I felt her arm push me to a halt and she moved me quickly behind a trader's cart. By now we were near the gates of the palace. I looked ahead and saw who she had seen. There, standing tall in conversation with a foot soldier was Uriah. I thought he had left at the break of dawn.

My feet stood fast, unwilling to move and moisture coated my hands. I stared at him. Even when he turned his head in my direction as though my eyes beckoned to him, I did not move nor did I hide. I wanted him to see me.

I tried to move towards him, but Anushka held me back. "Have mercy on him. If he lays his eyes on you, will he not carry a deeper burden of a longing unfulfilled to return to war?" I removed myself from her grip, angry at her words no matter how truthful they sounded. "Take your place!" I said using a harsher tone than I intended, and I walked away, reminding her that she was my slave. I walked swiftly leaving her behind not sure what I was going to do when I reached him. So many words floated through my mind, many possibilities. I walked quicker, trying to match the beat in my heart. Strength failed me but purpose carried me.

"Go back home, my Bathsheba, and take My peace with you." Yahweh's words halted me to stillness. I was not even praying yet He spoke. The tenderness with which the words came shocked me. "Yahweh, please, let me see him. I love him and I want to know that he loves me. My heart is wounded deep in me. I need You, Yahweh, help me obey or bring me to You, there is no peace on earth," I prayed and without tears too. I felt something different in the moment, desperate, hopeless, and empty. I needed something that I could hold on to, something more than the child within me. I felt spirit and soul at war within me: my will beckoned me forward, and my spirit urged me to obedience to Yahweh.

I was only a short distance away; enough to hear his words if I listened closely. All I had to do was mention his name loudly and he would hear me; he would turn around and he would see me. Before I took another step, Uriah removed his right hand from his pocket, raising it high and pointing towards the sky as he seemed to describe something to the soldier he spoke to. It was then I saw it: the purple cloth, my purple cloth, the one I had woven with red earthen twine, the one he wore on his horse in battle, the same one which now graced his pocket. He carried it with him.

My heart felt a rush of tender emotion, and, in that moment, he placed his right hand back into his pocket and held on to the cloth, caressing it gently before he replaced it. That left me unravelled - completely undone. I turned around and walked home. Fresh tears flowed and I let them. I now knew Uriah truly loved me. Yahweh had shown me.

I walked home slowly with Anushka taking careful steps behind me. She had waited where I left her watching me from a distance. I did not explain my tears, neither did I share with her what I had seen; that was mine to keep and cherish. When we got home, I stopped outside and stared at the rosebush. It was in full bloom and colours of red, pink, white and yellow flooded the earth. As I bent to pick one up, I felt the sharp prick of a thorn; I drew my thumb to my lips to soothe my sore skin. Suddenly, it occurred to me that my life was like a rose-bush: there was beauty and pain coexisting side by side.

I apologised to Anushka as soon as I entered the house. I had no need to have taken my frustration on her. I was raised to treat everyone with respect: free or slave, young or old. She had been a shoulder to lean on and my companion since the day I married; I did not want to lose her friendship; I had lost too much already.

That night, I did not bother to dress up in expectation of my husband's visit. I knew he was not coming. Especially when Anushka brought news that he had been summoned to eat and drink with the King. A fattened calf had been well roasted; and that plus four jugs of strong wine had been placed before the King and a few of his men including Uriah. Perhaps it was the King's last attempt to encourage him to go home. He knew that a well-fed man filled with wine would have a strong desire to be relieved by a woman. What the king did not know was that Uriah preferred to enjoy our moments with a clear mind. He enjoyed feasting and drinking in the company of men, but under his own roof he preferred well-watered wine and long conversations. Our nights were filled with much love, laughter and many words afterwards. Unlike a drunken man who lay with a woman and quickly fell asleep, Uriah was a very special man.

The news of Uriah's departure to Ammon did not come from Anushka. Midday had come and gone when a knock on the door caused me to put down the basket I was weaving and answer it. There stood two of the Kings' soldiers. I was petri-fied, a sudden flash back of the last time I was summoned.

"Are you the lady of the house?" The soldier to the left asked.

I nodded my head slowly.

"We bear gifts from Uriah," he said, and my heart slowed its fast breathing. There was no idle talk; they stepped aside in unison, revealing a heavy basket of food. I stepped aside as one of the soldiers carried it into the living quarters and the other placed a small pouch of sack cloth filled with coins in my hand. "He fares well and bids you well." And just like that, they turned and walked away.

Chapter Seventeen

I cannot recall how many days later, but it felt like only a few. I was outside my house dusting my sandals, having just returned from the market after a long morning of trading. I had decided to let my presence known for as many months as I could before I had to hide the child growing within me. I was not expecting any guests so the sharp knock on the door annoyed me. I wanted to rest as my body cried out for sleep. It seemed I needed sleep much more these days. I could hardly eat anything without the need to empty my stomach a few moments later. Only unleavened bread and mint tea stayed in my belly.

I decided to ignore the knock. Tilting my neck to the left and then the right to relieve the nagging ache, I sat down on my bed and rested my head on the wall. Shifting on the cold fabric, I attempted to relieve the itch in my skin. I sucked my cheeks to find moisture in my mouth but there was none. I needed to drink, to wash away the taste of the dream I had two nights ago. I had refused to think about it until that moment when the images came flooding back. As I allowed myself to remember, my eyes prickled, and my chest tightened. I remembered running into the forest in the dark of night, in an unfamiliar place. I had no knowledge of where I was running to, but I knew who I was running from. I kept screaming His name. "Yahwehhhhhhhhhhhhhh, no, no, no," was all I said. I turned my back on the only God I knew. The more I ran, the more I needed to run, for He was everywhere. His presence was everywhere. I wanted to hide but found no shelter. It felt like everywhere I stepped, He was there. I woke up petrified. I wiped the tears from my face and swallowed again to moisten my mouth. Still plagued by the meaning of my dream I was lost in my thoughts, staring outside the window as though the clouds held the answer to the mystery.

Only a few moments passed before Anushka burst into my room and threw herself at my feet wailing words I did not understand. I looked beyond the open door to see my grandfather Ahitophel and the King's soldiers. Rising slowly, I walked away from Anushka and straight to my grandfather's feet. I have loved this man my whole life but not as much as he has loved me; he often reminds me of this truth. My Saba would let me sit at his feet as a child and feed me the best portion of his meal. He lifted my face to his, urging me to rise and meet his gaze. He took my hands in his and squeezed them tightly, holding them like I was seven again. His eyes were wet. I looked for anger in his face; did someone tell him what the king did to me? Had Anushka betrayed me? Was he here to lead me to be stoned? So many questions flowed through my mind and even the wailing around me paled in my grandfather's continued silence. He just stared at me.

I urged his lips to move, and I think he willed this too. For a man who was never short of words, that day his words were few. I looked at his eyes again, searching for disappointment, but what I saw I did not understand.

Without thinking, I removed my hands from his and wrapped them around my belly, as though they had the power to protect this little one inside me. It was only five weeks since that shameful day. "Oh Lord, please give me many more months of life. Do not let me die with this child inside me." I whispered under my breath. I looked up as my Saba pulled my arms, urging me to take a seat on the wooden chair covered with sheep skin. I could see Anushka from the corner of my right eye; she was covering her mouth, hanging her head low. I shook my head in disappointment. The only thing I could imagine was that somehow, in their moment of passion, or perhaps after drinking too much wine, she had told Saba the truth.

I lifted my gaze to her, furious that hers was not to mine. Just outside my house, people had started to gather, and there sounded a chorus of wailing which made little sense, until Saba opened his mouth and spoke the words that deafened me almost instantly.

"Sheba, your husband has fallen at the hands of God's enemies. Uriah is dead"

The floor tilted and kept moving. I whirled around in circles and held my ears to stop the loud ringing so I could hear what was being said. I saw people's mouths moving, but all I could hear were the bells of war. Then the darkness came and took me away.

I woke up that evening in my own bed, drenched in sweat. A small lamp filled with rose oil burned in my room. Just outside my door, I heard the dirge being played, and I closed my eyes tightly. Pain burned through me. It was not a dream; I wished it was. I prayed it was. Uriah was dead. My husband was dead. I let out a soft wail, or so I thought. It was when the women who mourned rushed in to restrain me that I realised that I was screaming, and I was bound. My feet were tied with woven straw holding them in place. There was a sudden sting of rope against my skin that suggested my flesh had been cut.

"My lady, please have mercy on me." Anuskha held me down, her tears flowing without regard to what others might think. I looked around me to see my aunties, friends and some whom I did not recognise. Some in sack cloths, others with faces covered in ashes. I was already covered in a black gown which seemed to swallow me. I learned later that my aunty Sarai had brought it and covered me after I fell. What I did not understand was why I was bound. My head was heavier than my heart and disbelief left a bitter taste in my mouth. I tried to stand up, I needed some air. I needed to leave this place, and my body pushed me towards escape.

As though she could read my mind, Anushka grabbed hold of my garment. Still wailing, she whispered close enough and loud enough for my ears to finally respond, "Please, don't run, please have mercy, please remember...." She stopped.

So that is why I was bound - I had tried to run. I knew what she was going to say, and it was then I did remember. Yes, my husband was dead and that was what I wanted to be – DEAD. But there was a child to think of. "Untie me," I whispered to her. Our eyes met and understanding dawned. Relief flowed through me as I moved my legs. I welcomed the embrace of the women around me and, together, we wept!

Chapter Eighteen

The next few days of Shiva (the seven days of mourning) came and went quickly. I did not pray. I hardly spoke. I cried too many tears and finally gave in to well-watered wine to help me sleep. My dreams were filled of Uriah, some good, most bad. If I had known the last time I saw my husband at the palace gates would be the last time I would see him, I would have run to him. I would have not let fear, pride or anything else hold me bound; not even Yahweh's command would have kept me from speaking to him one last time. Even if Uriah felt honour-bound to not come to me, I would have broken every protocol and gone to him, not caring if it meant his anger burned towards me for my disobedience. It would not have mattered to me. I would have done it; I would have gone to him. Maybe, just maybe, he would have stayed home a few more days and he would have lived.

More news had come to Anushka's ears, and thus to mine, from the palace, thanks to the Israelite slave that fed the King. Uriah was killed the day after he returned to war. I could have saved him if I went to him. That burden sat with me, almost suffocating me. I placed my hand on what felt like a now empty head. My long black hair was gone. I had asked Anushka to cut it all off and she placed a black veil over my head.

As more days passed, the weight of my grief shifted from Uriah's permanent absence to my present predicament. What was going to become of my life? I was not just a widow, I was a pregnant, defiled widow. Uriah had no brother to redeem me. What would happen to this child? I still had many more days of mourning; even though I was now well into *sheloshim,* the thirty days of mourning.

By now, I could leave my house dressed in black cloth with my head covered, to try to re-integrate with the community, but I chose not to. I could not face anyone; I did not want to speak to anyone or see anything. I also could not trust myself not to run into the forest and wait for a wild beast to come and tear me apart or run into the depths of the Gihon and allow the water to swallow me. I had imagined so many ways to take my own life, but for the child I carried inside of me, I knew I would have. Perhaps, Adonai placed him within me to preserve me.

Many more days passed before I could finally pray. At first, all I could say was, "Adonai." I knew Him as Yahweh, but I remembered the way my father had screamed "ADONAIIIIII" the day my mother died. Grief had caused me to change the way I spoke His name or thought of Him. Adonai, my God who had dealt me a wicked, painful blow. My God who had abandoned me to suffer the weight of a sin that was not mine. I still wanted to pray; I wanted to take this pain somewhere to someone. I did not want to turn to false gods, even though I saw the wooden God Anushka put beside my bed, telling me it would bring rest to my weary soul. I pushed her and the wooden creature away.

My heart was fixed on the God of Israel. But that God, I spoke to as Yahweh, the one I called merciful and kind, He felt so far away now. "Adonai!" I whispered. The name felt more befitting. I knew it was the same God, but the name-change helped me talk to Him but not as my Yahweh.

"Why did you take him? Why did you let him die?" I prayed with no response. My heart was angry towards Adonai - bitter, cold and heavy. That night, as I lay down to sleep, I felt a presence around me. I recalled the dream I had weeks ago where I was running from Yahweh and the harder I ran, the more I kept running into Him because He was everywhere. I felt that same presence around me, right in my room. Then, as though to confirm it, I saw a tiny glow, not as bright as it was the first time, but a twinkle nonetheless — a firefly. It was dancing just beyond the edge of my bed, out of my reach but within my sight. Warmth filled my heart and a flicker of joy for the first time in weeks rushed in. Adonai was with me.

I fell to my knees and began to pray. "Help me, Adonai. Help me. I do not know what to do or what will become of me. Speak to Your servant. Save Your child within me. Protect my father and the other men at war. Comfort my heart......" The words kept tumbling out and I could not stop praying about anything and everything. No tears flowed — just words; some I could understand, others were like groans or pain-filled whispers. I must have fallen asleep while praying as I found myself in what looked like the Lord's Garden. It was beautiful, filled with many flowers. I drank the scent of them, desperate to taste the beauty that lay before me.

There were red, green and sunlight yellow flowers scattered everywhere. There were huge butterflies and tiny birds singing as though in praise. It was like nothing I had ever seen or heard described before. It was beautiful.

As I ran through the fields, I felt like a child, touching everything along the way. I heard the stream even before I saw it. Flowing majestically, the water fell from the heavens and flowed into a small river where I dared to step. I inhaled peace, I wanted to stay here forever. I looked around and saw no one, which confused me as I could hear music; only then did I see it was the trees that clapped a tune, the leaves making a melody to which the birds danced. In the far distance, I saw two turtle doves sitting on the branch of a huge tree. They held something that glistened in their beaks. I stood in awe at the wonder and beauty around me. Intrigued by the doves I walked towards them; they were on the other side of the river. I skipped towards the far side, where the water seemed shallow and I could see the rocks that sat beneath. As I moved closer, I stopped as my face glistened in the water, I saw myself, in my house, on my knees, with my veil over my head calling out to Adonai. I was confused and panic arrested me. Was I dead? Is this heaven? How can I see myself there and I am here? I looked around me hastily, and then leaned down to touch the water, trying to touch me, instead, I heard me: "Why did this happen to me? What will become of me? Adonai, please help me." My own prayers carried through the water into the place of beauty.

A rustling of leaves made me look up and I watched a flock of lambs run across the huge field in the distance. And then, I looked up skywards to see two doves fly towards me: one on the left, the other on the right, both holding in their beaks, a band made of gold set with red rubies encircling it. It was the most beautiful thing I had ever seen. I stared in wonder as they flew above me and then rested it on my head. Immediately, I opened my eyes.

I gasped for air suddenly, unable to breathe as I tried to adjust my sight to the darkness around me. My modest bedroom paled in comparison to the paradise that I had just left. I grabbed my veil tightly, shaking back and forth on the floor where I still knelt. Had I just seen a vision? This was more than a dream. I did not understand it. My right hand, the hand with which I reached into the river, was wet. Though my mind tried to tell me it was river water, the sweat on my forehead brought me back to the reality that my hand had been a cloth instead of my veil. Yet, the dream felt so real. Still shaken, I climbed into bed and immediately fell asleep. I had had enough for one night.

I spent the next few days trying to understand the meaning of this vision. I even went to the front garden to try to relive the memories by sniffing the rosebush. I could not share this with anyone — not any of my friends who came to sit with me, nor even my aunty, nor Anushka. I just kept it in my heart and called out to Adonai as often as I could. My period of mourning was almost done; in my opinion, thirty days was not long enough. No time is long enough to recover from such pain. Maybe for a man, it was easier.

My Aunt Sarai, my mother's older sister, floated into my consciousness. When her husband died in battle, she was given to his younger brother on the thirty-third day after he was buried. At the time, I said to myself, I could never do that. I did not say it aloud within hearing distance of my mother and the other women who waited on her to prepare her for the wedding. I was barely eleven years old at the time but already had a rebellious heart towards our customs and tradition. Aunty Sarai had been married to her cousin Caleb for many years, even before I was born. It seemed so crazy to me that she was given in marriage to his brother Matthew who was many years younger than she was; especially a man who already had two wives and several concubines. A few days after their marriage, the day I turned twelve years, my mother took the time to explain the purpose of the tradition. She told me that it was done to protect both the woman and her husband's lineage. She said the life of a widow, especially one without sons, was a fate worse than death. Under the roof of her husband's brother, Aunty Sarai would find protection as she had no sons. Otherwise, she would end up destitute. I recoiled as I suddenly thought of my own fate, a defiled, pregnant widow.

Chapter Nineteen

Exactly twenty-three days after the news of my husband's death reached me, I felt as though I had made up my mind what to do next. I needed to get away. It would soon be time for me to go and present myself falsely at the Mikveh; the cycles were moving quickly. I could not continue to live this lie. I was desperate to protect my child. My new plan was to sell everything I owned, take the sack of coins and move far away from Jerusalem, perhaps as far as Rome. I would leave the home I had always known and buy passage on a boat to anywhere else. If I was going to become a destitute widow, I would much rather beg amongst strangers than my own people. I would do anything to keep this innocent child alive and free from the wickedness of this world. Once the child was born and weaned, I would send him back with Anushka to be laid at his father's feet.

When I called Anushka to share my plans with her, I intended only to share the part about running away. Yet, the vision tumbled out of my mouth, word-for-word, in exactly the way it happened. I was stunned at my own recollection. As the tale unfolded, I relived the moment; I lived through the experience again as if I was back in that paradise. I could sense the presence of Adonai, just like it was that day, and I even felt the weight of the gold band on my now growing hair.

"What does it mean, this vision?" She asked me, shaking her head to the same rhythm I shook mine.

"I do not know, Nush... But whatever it means, I know that Adonai has spoken," I whispered.

"I have heard of a merchant ship coming next week from Tyre into the waters of the Mediterranean Sea, to the far west of Israel. It will take a day's journey by foot to reach it and many silver coins to buy passage. But that is not all that is at stake: without the company of a man, we could be taken as slaves and used as concubines on the boat." Her words carried the weight of wisdom.

Two women, with a sack full of coins, travelling alone was an invitation for trouble. I felt deflated as realisation dawned.

"Every day this child grows within me, there are fewer days left until I am exposed. Wherever we must go to hide, let us go." My words urgent, I tugged at her hand as though it would prompt a response.

We sat looking at each other in silence. I had lived in Jerusalem all my life and knew no other place, save for the stories from battlefields and through the eyes of Uriah. But all the places he spoke of were places he went to fight the Lord's enemies; these were not places I could run to for shelter. "What about Egypt, should we go back to your home?"

Shaking her head vigorously, Anushka spoke barely above a whisper. "I was sold into slavery as a child by my own uncle.

He killed my father, taking my mother as his own wife. I pleaded with her to help me; to save me, but she sat in silence as I was sold for only a few brown coins. What do I know of Egypt besides pain?" Despair loomed in the air, hanging over us like lowering clouds.

"Is there no one from my master's household — brother, cousin or family member — that will redeem you? The baby is still within many months of being born; if you are wedded soon, perhaps the truth of the child can still be hidden. Some babies are known to be born before their time; the weeks can be counted short. Besides, you should now be coming out of your uncleanness; the time would be ripe if you are redeemed, and hope will arise for the child."

At Anushka's words, a renewed hope shimmered, almost palpably before me. Yes, my mourning was due to end soon, but no one had yet come forward to express a desire to redeem me. Uriah was a Hittite. If he had any family, they would be far away and unknown to me. I was young and my beauty was rumoured near and far. Had there been a redeemer amongst my husband's own, he would have been hard pressed to refuse me.

It seemed like God had so many ways of saving me, yet each time a solution presented itself, the door slammed shut. If Uriah had only come home, if he had obeyed the King's instructions, even if for just one night, this child would have been saved. I would have been spared the certain pain of the future that stretched before me. A hatred for the King twisted my soul. I had received no words from him, not even condolences for my husband's death. Uriah was one of his mighty thirty. I looked outside the open door; in the distance I could see the palace. I turned back to Anushka and said, "Surely a word to his grieving widow is not out of place; a word to his wife that he defiled and filled with his seed is only right." I tossed my veil to the ground, stamping on it multiple times for no reason other than to relieve the anger that worked its way through me like a plague.

My Saba had been to visit me many times and not once had he mentioned a word from the King, not even a basket of food had filled our home from the palace. The rejection was painful; it felt like my husband's memory was thrown on the floor and died alongside his body and my hopes and dreams. The sacrifice he made for the King was seemingly without reward.

That same night before I slept, I prayed, "Adonai, will You not honour Your son? He fought for You not just for King David. Please honour his death."

That night, I dreamt of Uriah. I saw him holding his hands towards heaven, and it was filled with fireflies. Laughter lit his handsome face as he looked at the tiny creatures with delight. Beside him, another figure with a face I could not see was standing, dressed in a white tunic, a bright light flowing from him.

Together they played with these tiny creatures. He was at peace; he laughed whilst I cried. It seemed he was in the better place, and I was grateful for the glimpse of him. I looked up at heaven and said Yahweh!

The last few days of my mourning were filled with unmet expectation. Without realising it, each time I heard footsteps at the door, I was hoping for news of a redeemer. Old or young, I would not care, just someone that would take away the shame of widowhood and save my unborn child.

No one came!

Chapter Twenty

At the end of my *sheloshim* I went to the mountain Moriah. Thirty days came and went so quickly. Even though my life had stopped, it seemed like life around me kept moving. Babies were being born, marriages happened and, yes, there was one or maybe two more deaths. But everyone seemed to just continue living and I was barely existing.

The need to be closer to God drew me to the huge mountain. It was not a quick journey by foot, so I left just at the break of dawn, praying as I walked. Heading away from the city, I headed towards what some now called the Old Jerusalem since the City of David had been built at the heart of the city now called the New Jerusalem. It was to the top of this mountain that our father Abraham had taken his son Isaac to sacrifice to the Lord. That was one of my favourite stories, one I heard from my father's mouth.

I was still a little girl when my Abba told me how God had tested Abraham's faith and obedience. He asked him to sacrifice his son. Without fear, he took the boy all the way up to

BECOMING QUEEN BATHSHEBA · 95

Mount Moriah and just as he was about to slay him, the Lord himself stopped him and provided a lamb to be sacrificed in his place. I wondered if I would have had the faith to be so obedient, to trust God so fully. I longed for that; I needed that type of courage.

If Yahweh was to be found, He would be on Mount Moriah, so I hastened my step. When I arrived at the foot of the mountain, I stared up at the slow ascent. I had no intention of climbing to the top, it would take days. I found a cool spot, away from the traders who followed the route that led outside Jerusalem. As a woman dressed in black sackcloth, I was obviously mourning. I knew I would hardly be disturbed. By now, the sun had risen, and daylight flooded the land as sweet morning scents filled the air.

I sat on the ground, silent, with my veil covering my hair and wept for my husband, the pain of my loss clutching at my chest. I missed the life we had. I missed the big things as well as the little things. Even the things I disliked — the thunder of his snoring, with mouth wide open after a good meal and a jug of wine; the sucking of his teeth while he ate his meal; the way he tapped the floor with his left foot; and even the loud expel of air that forced me to open the windows wide. I missed those things even as much as I missed the tenderness of his kisses on my skin. "Oh Yahweh, will love never fill my heart and warm my bones again?" I cried, ashamed to be hungry for the tender touch of Uriah.

The last memory I had of being with a man was not only painful, but it was also shameful. Will that be the memory that I die with? "Uriah, why did you leave me?" I spoke to the earth as though he heard. My God was Yahweh again. After He had shown me Uriah in a dream, smiling with hands filled with light, I knew that he was at peace and this brought me comfort. My God had not forsaken him; my God will not forsake me.

A few hours passed and I set the picnic of bread and fish before me; the one I had hurriedly thrown together by the early morning light. I stuffed the food into my mouth and drank deeply. The wine skin of cool water was now empty beside me, and I closed my eyes for a minute to rest. Then, it was time to head back home. I had no idea what the next few days were going to be, but I knew that I had to go to the Mikveh at some point, after which I would resume trading in public for as many months as my clothes could hide the growing child inside me.

That evening, the thirty-first day after the news of my husband's death, I walked home, my heart heavy and filled with emotions. As I drew closer, I spotted the King's chariot outside my house. One of the horses had its nose weeding my rosebush. Bile rose to my lips as I recognised the chariot. It was the same one that I rode from the palace that night or at least, it looked very similar. I had no idea how many chariots the King owned, but I knew he was a man of great wealth. This could well be one of thousands. Straining my eyes to see further into the distance in the last of the light of day, I examined it. To me, it looked like the same one I had ridden in around the same time about two months before. A quiet thought fleeted through my mind: was my father dead? The war seemed to rage on and only last week, more news of fallen soldiers had reached the city. I walked quicker, praying that all was well, seeing no good reason why the King's chariot was outside my house.

Anushka rushed towards me as soon as she saw me appear. She grabbed my feet, and I could see she had been crying. Still kneeling, she held in her hands four statues, three of the same female god and the fourth of something I did not recognise. It looked to be some kind of animal. I watched in shock as she threw one after the other into the road ahead of me, shouting words I could not understand. After the fourth god was flung, she bowed down and said, "I beg you to lead me to your God: the one you call on and hears you, the one who speaks to you in dreams and visions; for now I know." She paused, beating her chest hard, with tears flowing down her eyes. "Now I know, He is a true God, and He is the God I want to worship."

It was then I saw my Saba at the door. A smile rested on his face. His hand bore the weight of the bag he carried and, even before I reached him, I could see the fine clothes and jewellery that overflowed the five baskets next to his feet.

I knelt down to greet him, grateful for his company but intrigued by his entourage as well as his demeanour. "Peace be unto you, my child. Rise to your feet and rejoice for today the God of Israel has visited the household of Uriah." With that, he placed a heavy gold bracelet on my right arm and then on my left. He also picked up a red veil, woven with precious stone and placed it on my head. I turned to look at Anushka as well as the small crowd that now gathered around the chariot. I was confused, wondering what was happening. And then, I saw Aunt Sarai. In her hand she had a basket, the one used for ceremonial preparation, marriage preparation.

My mouth dropped wide open and before I could even ask, my Saba knelt and placed another chain on my left foot and placed before me a small purple rug. Pointing at the rug, he said, "Take your place Bathsheba for the King himself has redeemed you."

Chapter Twenty-One

A wave of nausea rushed through me. It was too late in the evening for it to be the baby; this child only caused my stomach to turn in the early hours. This wave of sickness I felt was because of the weight of the word my ears heard. I repeated them in my mind, shock holding me captive and unable to take one step.

THE KING HIMSELF WANTS TO REDEEM ME? Is he crazy?

My head fell into my hands as I bellowed from my soul. "Oh Adonai, anyone else but him, no, no, no, I will die first before I marry that man." I did not whisper, the words dared to spring loudly from my mouth shocking my grandfather to the place where he now stood.

"Should I dig a grave near your mother's then, Sheba? The king does not ask, he demands." He pulled me onto the purple rug sealing my fate. It was not that I had a choice, as Saba said, it was not a request; this was not a proposal.

My Saba cleared his throat to get my attention, so I looked at him. "Uriah has bound you to thinking that marriage is about love. I know the love you had for him. I too loved him like my own son and each day I praised Yahweh that my Sheba was given to a man who honoured her much more than even I as a man honoured any of my own wives. Uriah is now gone. Put aside your pain and take shelter within the palace walls. There is no greater fate any woman can desire than under the protection of the King. He does this to honour me, to honour your father and your husband. Can you not see the hand of the almighty God on your head, Sheba? Can you not see it? Prepare now, in the morning, you will be joined with the King." Kissing my forehead, he retreated to the King's chariot and left.

The next few hours were filled with noise, wine and laughter as the women in my house started to prepare me for the wedding the next morning. Six slave girls were sent from the palace and four guards stood outside the door. It made no sense to have this excessive protection. I had lived in this same house with no trouble for more years than I wanted to count. What was suddenly going to befall me overnight that I needed the protection of armed guards outside my house? It was at the Kings' orders.

It felt too much. It was all too much. The gifts he had sent, the fabrics, the food, it was overwhelming. I knew I was hardly going to sleep that night. Usually, brides were soaked in scented oils months before the wedding; it took several weeks to scrub the skin and brush the hair, even more weeks to sew the fabric. All these things we now had mere hours to do. Although a widow's remarriage was not as glamorous as a virgin bride, it was still a marriage and preparations were important, but we had no time. It was as if King David woke up that morning and suddenly decided to marry me: what the King wanted, the King got! So, now I would spend many hours, awake, getting ready for that man.

I did not even want to say his name: he had robbed me of so much already and now he was robbing me of sleep. The precious moment I had at the mountain with Yahweh seemed like a distant memory now; as though my spirit wanted to rebel, I called out, "Adonai," and not in a loving way.

The continued chatter of the women around me started to grate on me. I did not want to hear words like blessed, chosen or lucky. I felt none of that. Anushka joined them in the songs of joy, all of them happy to prepare me for marriage to the King. They ate, they drank, and they worked.

With the excuse that I wanted to relieve myself in the back house, I managed to slip into Uriah's bed chamber from the corner of the house. I needed some space to think, to be alone for only a few moments. I played back the conversation with my Saba, the question he asked still fresh in my mind. Could I not see God's hand in this? No, I could not. Where was the hand of Adonai in this? Where? Should I be joined to the man who took me at his will, a man who already had six or seven wives and numerous concubines? A man who had no heart towards me. How could God's hand be in this?

This was not my prayer; this was not my dream. The life I had with Uriah was what I craved — one man, one wife, one slave, and many children. That was my heart's cry. To be joined with a man who loved me, a man whom I loved and treated like *my* king even though he was not the King. I knew my Saba was right. What I had with Uriah was not commonplace. There were not many men who had taken only one wife. Even our father Abraham had once taken his Egyptian slave as wife. Maybe in time, Uriah too would have taken other wives as well. I was naïve to think otherwise. Marriage was not about love. Marriage was not about punishment either. Yet, this felt like I was being punished.

"Is there any wrong in me, Adonai? Search my heart and show me: is there any wrong in me? Do you hear me? Do you even answer me? Is your hand in this?" I screamed through clenched teeth, my heart breaking inside me.

A touch on my shoulder turned my attention to my Aunt Sarai who must have heard me scream.

"What troubles you, my child? Why is your countenance so sad? Is there anything too hard for our God who has heard my prayers?"

I grabbed her open arm and wept into it, allowing her words to wash over me. Her prayers? She has been praying for me? For this fate?

"I still love him, Aunty. How can I be given to another? It is too soon; my heart grieves still!"

I felt her push my hair away from the side of my face.

"I know how you feel, my child. Love and time don't always agree. I still miss my Caleb even though many years have gone by; and you will still miss Uriah even till you take your last breath. But life, it is for those who live. And love for the King, even though it feels far away, will come. God has dealt kindly with you; you have been redeemed by the king, Bathsheba, favour rests upon you. Now you are blinded with sorrow, I understand that, but take heart. It will be well with you. Just give it some time in prayer."

I welcomed her warm embrace, I needed it.

Aunt Sarai placed her hands on my head, running her fingers through my hair in a way that brought me comfort, and I began to relax and breathe easier.

"When my Caleb died," she continued, "I felt like a part of me died as well. As you know, I too was redeemed by his younger brother who already had wives and concubines. They were not kind to me; the first few years were miserable, especially when my hands remained empty of a child. But then, God filled me with sons and daughters, and, in His time, my mourning turned to laughter. I know that in time God will bless you with the sons of the King and, from them, joy will come; and one day, when the King calls for you, love will replace duty and your body will welcome his embrace. In time and with prayer this too shall come to be. As my Lord Ahitophel said, look Bathsheba and see the hand of God in this thing."

No sooner had the words left her mouth than the vision I had many days ago flashed through my mind. I immediately remembered the two white doves and placed my hand on my head, at the exact spot where I felt them place the gold band with rubies. Now it started to make sense; Yahweh had already pre-warned me, I just did not understand the vision. I remembered the beauty of the garden, and the peace that flowed from the river; and that same peace now settled within me. Yahweh knew. And Anushka knew and understood even before I did myself. I looked at my Aunt Sarai and allowed a small smile to stain my face. If only she knew the truth of her words. Well, some of it, because I was already carrying a son for the King and yet, God's hand was upon me. But love? That is not possible. I will never love King David. That was what my heart believed.

Morning came much quicker than I anticipated. Many hands made the preparations light and I felt grateful for the slave girls sent from the palace as my preparation was completed quickly, meaning we all had time for a few hours' sleep. By now, my hair was well soaked in honey; it was easy because it was much shorter than the waist long hair that I had carried for years. Fresh goat milk had been poured in a large basin for my body and hair to be soaked in. Anushka had woken before the sun to warm the milk over large wooden pots and add fragrant oils from the baskets sent from the palace. These ones teased my nostrils with unfamiliar yet rich scents; scents I had never previously experienced. One, in particular, was rich yet fruity, both delicate and strong. My stomach rumbled in response, thinking it was to be fed.

I looked over to see my wedding veil now beautifully complete with expensive purple stones decorating the hem. A long purple gown had also been sewn overnight by many talented hands and was laid out ready to be worn. I did not know what time the chariot would arrive, but I knew that I would be ready — the women were already seeing to that. The house was again filled with cheerful chatter and the giggling told me some of the slave girls were already high on wine.

As I lay in the warm bath, Anushka washed my hair, taking time to massage my scalp; I rested into the pleasure of it and luxuriated in the heady scent of the fragranced oils. It soothed me and gave rest to my mind.

"Yahweh already planned all this, and we were worrying? You do serve a wonderful God," she whispered and before I could respond, she started to sing. It gave me the time to think of what Yahweh had done.

"He has covered your shame and protected this child, my lady."
She sang the words softly.

"Anushka," I said, interrupting her tune, wanting her full
attention. "Can this child be truly protected? A woman's way is
nine months. I would only be seven months within the palace
before this child is born. Words will be spoken." I reminded her
quietly to keep the words between only us.

"No, my lady, only we know this to be so. No one knows the
way of God and how he counts the months for birth. I have
seen with my owns eyes women bring forth ten months and
some even six or seven, though it is hard for the babies who are
so early to be born in good health. The time is not too far gone
and the King knows of the matter. Rest now, for your God has
shown His favour and it is on this account that I placed aside
all other Gods to worship Yahweh." She paused to pour
fragrant milk on my hair before continuing. "Did you not tell
me of your vision where two doves placed a crown of gold
upon your head? And tell me now, in only a few hours, will the
King himself not appoint you? Is this not the work of the Lord?
Put aside your fears and rejoice, for both your life and the life of
this child has been redeemed."

At the conclusion of her words, I closed my eyes in prayer. She
increased the power of her voice in song allowing the melody
to float into the main house.

Chapter Twenty-Two

When the chariots finally came, I was already dressed, covered from head to toe in the finest, softest garment my skin had ever known. The scent of that mysterious oil settled upon me. I liked it. It reminded me of the fragrance of the Garden of Yahweh, the one where the wildflowers grew and the trees clapped in melody. It was not until the chariot graced the palace walls that it occurred to me that not only was I going to marry the King, but for the next seven days, I would be locked away with the king in his inner chambers. My blood ran cold as I remembered the last time I was alone with him. Only few words were spoken though painful memories were created; and now, I was going to come face to face with him again. What would I say?

Panic rippled through me, and I felt as if air was in short supply. My breathing quickened and I gasped trying to find relief, but there was none. I rested my head on the carriage wall as I fought to ease my breathing. The last time I felt like this, I was Eight years old. I had gone to play with the baby lambs that were born a few days previously. They were in the green field behind our home, the one my father had told me so many times not to go to. It belonged to a wealthy merchant, a fierce man who traded in cattle and wheat. This man had many disagreements with my father over land, because he knew him to be a man of war. Each time my father travelled, he encroached a bit more into my father's own land, planting and harvesting from it without sharing any profit. My father did not like this man, especially after he had spoken against my mother.

I had seen the tiny lambs and longed to cuddle them, so that afternoon I snuck out the back door, passed the bath house, climbed the small fence, and went to play with the lambs. I enjoyed their company and watched as they nursed from their mother and two of the babies climbed into my open hands.

I was only there for a few moments, and all seemed to be well, but when I left the lambs, I forgot to close the gate behind me. By the time I realised what I had done, there were cattle everywhere, running around the planted fields and eating wheat waiting to be harvested. When the matter was reported to my father, it was the look he gave me that brought out the same panic that I was now experiencing in the king's chariot. He did not hold back the rod from me as his anger made its mark on my back. It cost him half of his wages to replace what was lost that day. As I relived that painful memory, the familiarity of the panic left my mouth bitter and dry.

My *Saba* awaited me at the entrance of the King's palace. He walked ahead of me into the King's court where a group of courtiers had gathered to bear witness to the union. The ceremony was carried out in a smaller room, just outside the King's throne room. I did not raise my head to take note of all the people that were present that day; I vaguely remember seeing some of the King's wives and a few city officials and then, finally, the King himself.

King David stood tall, dressed in a deep purple robe, the same shade of the purple rug my Saba laid at my feet the previous day and the same shade of my gown. It looked like the fabric had been cut from the robe itself. His dark red hair flowed freely under his crown and he looked taller and larger than I remembered. I could not, would not, meet his eyes. I was grateful for the veil that covered my face and even when he raised it to look at me after the words were spoken by the priest, my eyes were closed. I could not bring myself to look at him.

The ceremony was over quickly, and the musicians played loudly as the palace bustled with life. Food was plenty and many well-wishers filled the grounds. The town criers had gone out before sunrise to announce to the people that the King was getting married that day. Even before the town criers returned from the length and breadth of Jerusalem, the palace grounds started filling with people shouting, "Long live the King".

After the ceremony, I was escorted into the King's living quarters and beyond the outer court, the large dining room table groaned with food set out for a meal for two. On the other side was a door through which I glimpsed a huge bed and another room beyond. I was shocked to see that this was not the same chambers I had been entertained in a few short months ago. This place, although within the palace walls, was different. I could not find my bearings. I had heard it said the palace was enormous, and now I saw it for myself. I did not know whether I stood in the North or South wing. My gaze flickered around me, searching the place that was to be my new home.

Raw emotion flooded me, the strongest being panic that refused to leave. It gripped me tighter than the corset I was so desperate to remove. I had begged Anushka not to bind it too tight, but she did not listen and now I could barely catch a breath. Three slave girls, also dressed in ceremonial attire, led me into the bedroom and undressed me. I would again be cleansed and dressed in a lighter robe before the King arrived. "Where is Anushka?" I asked, not willing to be attended to by anyone other than her.

"The king's private chambers will not be defiled by Egyptian slaves, my mistress," one of the girls replied. She had kind eyes and her smile immediately put me at ease. "I am Naomi, daughter of Hosea the town silversmith. I will serve you, my lady," and she bowed before me.

The other girls nimbly started laying out clothes and preparing a bath, as they hung on Naomi's every word.

"When will I see Anushka?" I asked, desperate to have the ear of my confidant again and to have some sort of normalcy in my life. I was used to having one slave and sometimes it felt like one too many, but the three girls running around me, and fussing pounded on my brain harder than the drummers at a mourning ceremony.

"Once the seven days are completed and the king escorts you to your chambers, you may be re-joined by your Egyptian slave at the discretion of the king." There was something in her words that left me unsure about whether Anushka would be a part of my future. Was this my life now? At the discretion of the king? I shivered at the thought. I needed her, not just for my own peace of mind, but for the plans we had for the baby.

Chapter Twenty-Three

As I allowed myself to be primed and pampered again, only a few hours after the first soaking in goat's milk, I wondered what the next seven days with the king would be like. I did not expect an explanation or an apology, but the walls would not be filled with silence. So, what words would be spoken? Would he expect me to lay with him again at his will? What would the king do with me tonight?

Hours passed and King David had not yet arrived in his quarters. I later heard that he was walking throughout the palace and grounds, receiving gifts from the people who came to celebrate his union. Custom dictated he walked around the courtyard twice, acknowledging not only the people, but God. He would then sit in counsel with his leaders before he could retreat into the inner chambers for the next seven days alone with me to feast. Whilst we feasted inside, outside, in the palace court yards, there would be simultaneous feasting and drinking for the next seven days.

The wedding to the king was completely unlike my wedding to Uriah. Many more words were spoken and more witnesses, including my Saba, were present. The priests performed additional rites: some, I understood; others, I just heard and spoke the words I was asked to speak. All glory was given to Yahweh as our hands were bound together with a cord. I was lost in my own thoughts throughout the whole ceremony, though I vaguely remembered at least seven prayers were said and the king placed not one but two rings on my left middle finger and placed yet another gold bangle on my right wrist. I flinched as the king removed one of the rings from his finger and placed it on mine. Eyeing it suspiciously and wondering if it was the same ring that had left a mark on my inner arm, I removed it the minute I was alone.

When the king finally arrived, I was asleep on the long velvet chair that stretched in front of the huge window. I had been looking out into the streets. They were filled with the people of Jerusalem for as far as my eyes could see. They packed every inch of the street and, I imagined, every other street. The news of the wedding spread fast and wide. I was still tired from the night before, so I closed my eyes, listening to the music that filled the city and must have drifted off into a deep sleep.

I felt Naomi's hand on my shoulder, attempting to shake me awake; and then a cold hand brushed my cheek.

"Leave us," the king said loudly.

I listened as light feet retreated from the room. My heart slowed to a steady beat; even I could feel it trying to escape from my mouth. My eyes still tightly shut I lay there waiting.

"Is it your desire not to look at me or speak to me for the rest of your time?" His voice whispered in my ears; his breath warm against my skin. I did not know what to say or even what my desire actually was. I opened my eyes slowly, assuming he had moved away from me, even if only a little, but instead, my eyes met his and we stayed locked-in in that moment. Though only a few minutes, it felt like hours passed and discomfort creeped slowly up and down my back as sourness filled my mouth.

Chapter Twenty-Four

King David stood above me and held out his hand. "Rise, my queen, let us feast." For a moment I stared, his words striking my heart – My Queen! His queen? I placed my hand in his and allowed him to guide me to the table, taking my seat where he stopped. As though the king sensed my hesitation, he walked to the far corner of the banquet room and spoke to one of the guards on the other side of the door. A short while later, a small man arrived, carrying a huge basket. He wore a grey lined cloth and red robes of a priest or eunuch. I knew not which. By this time, the king was sitting on the table next to me and waited for the man to arrive at the table. His short legs made the journey seem longer than it should have been.

When he got to the table, he placed the basket at the king's feet and immediately bowed down before him, kissing the ground three times. King David opened the basket and lifted out an elaborate purple box encrusted with precious jewels. He opened it and turned it towards me. In the box lay a gold crown. It was much smaller than the other crowns I had seen that day at the wedding, but it was beautiful. It had leaves of rose petals all around it, each leaf had a huge sparkling white stone at its tip. On the sides of the crown, both left and right, sat a golden dove. My eyes watered at the sight of them.

King David dismissed the crown bearer. When he lifted the veil from my head, I saw his eyes widen in shock and then he lifted my face to his. "You cut off your hair, Bathsheba! Are you not a free woman? Why did you burden yourself to mourn like a captive?"

I do not know what pained me more: the way he said my name or his calling my choice a burden. My heart was burdened, my husband was dead at war. You should be the one who is dead, I almost screamed. I hated that he wanted to dictate the way I should mourn, or maybe it was the words of Naomi, "At the king's discretion," that still rang in my ears.

Without thinking, I pushed his hand away from me, turning my face to the ground. Let him kill me, I did not care. The King stood before me not moving. I heard him breath and I waited to feel the weight of his hand against my cheek. Instead, I felt the weight of the crown touch my head as he gently placed it upon me. I looked up then even as tears mixed with kohl left black rivulets on my cheeks. King David stared at me, his eyes slightly red; then he whispered, "My queen," and walked away.

I sat alone in the banquet room. My stomach grumbled in the stillness reminding me that I had not eaten all day. There was plentiful food in front of me, yet I knew I could not eat until the king had eaten. I waited and waited, hoping he would return, but deep down, I knew he would not. I had scorned him. "Yahweh, help me. What am I to do? I know not what to do or what to say. Please help me," I prayed earnestly.

As I stood up, I wiped hands wet from my face on my garment and paced around the room. I walked towards the door, opened it, and peered out to see the king standing at the window on the other side of the room. There was a glass of wine in his hand and a half empty jug on the table next to where he stood.

"*Go to your king.*" The voice came to me like a gentle whisper, one I chose to ignore. Again, it came. "*Go to your husband.*" Again, I ignored it. My head betrayed me with words that my heart did not want to hear, the last word more annoying than the first. He may be my king, but my husband? That was too much for me to swallow. This was not Uriah; this was not my husband.

"*Bathsheba!*" My name rang within my skull; it sounded so loud that I turned to look around, almost dancing in circles in my haste to find out who had spoken it.

Who called me? I was alone. Swift movement caused the crown on my head to wobble, and I reached to steady it. As I touched the crown, I felt the dove and remembered. It was slightly raised and felt smooth to the touch making it easy to define every element of the beautiful bird as I rubbed it gently.

"*Go to your king.*" This time my legs seemed to move independently of my thoughts, and I walked towards the king not knowing what I was going to say or if he was going to listen.

Chapter Twenty-Five

As he heard me approach, he turned to me and smiled. I fell to the ground, my gaze on the floor. No matter what I thought or how I felt, he was still the king and I needed to respect this fact and remember it always. To disobey him or stand in any kind of defiance not only meant my death, but an enemy of the king was also an enemy of Yahweh. He was God's chosen one.

"I beg your forgiveness my King. Look upon your maidservant with the Lord's mercy." I waited for a response, but none came. The king just stood unmoving. I knelt before him as many moments passed and my knees started to wobble beneath me. I waited and listened to the sound of the wine sliding down his throat, gulp after gulp. I could almost feel his eyes burn my skin. Still, he said and did nothing. After waiting longer than one woman could bear, I finally decided to sneak a peek. Was he still looking at me? Was I being punished on my knees like a little child? When I finally raised my eyes and opened them, I saw the King's right hand before me. My husband had been standing there, drinking with his left hand and waiting for me to take his right. While I knelt there with my eyes closed, looking at the ground, he was standing there with his hand outstretched to me, waiting for me while I was waiting for him.

I immediately grabbed his outstretched hand and he pulled me towards him. Over a head taller than me, it was necessary for me to tilt my head upwards to look him in the eye. I felt so small next to him. Even as he stared at me, I turned away quickly unable to hold his gaze — besides, it was rude to stare.

"Why do you shift your eyes away from me, my queen? Does your heart burn with so much anger towards me? Did you not want me to redeem you?" He paused waiting for a response, when none left my lips, he continued. "I have heard of your love for Uriah and the way you have mourned him these past few days. I have now seen that love myself in your shaven head and your continued mourning for him. I did what I could to reunite you when I summoned him home from war. He refused to go home, even against my command. Tell me, are you still with child?" The last word was a whisper.

I nodded my head in response and as though the child wanted to signify his presence, my stomach growled loudly.

"Let us feast," the king said, and for the second time that day, he took me to the banquet table. This time, we sat and ate, albeit in silence.

Relief washed over me as my hunger was eased and my stomach settled. Only then did I hear the music that played softly outside the door. A few moments later a sharp knock was heard on that same door, followed by the entrance of Naomi and a few other slaves, coming to clear the empty bowls and fill the room with more food. Just then, my eyes made contact with a girl I had not seen before. She smiled and nodded as she brought in fresh fruits and a silver jug filled with mint tea. As she set the tea before me, I immediately knew who she was — the meal bearer, the one that had been bringing word to Anushka from the king's court.

When most of the dishes had been cleared, and the king stepped into the inner bed chamber, she rushed over to me and quickly introduced herself as Eliana. "My queen, Anushka remains in the palace ground waiting for word from you. How do you fare?" She asked. She was the first person, aside from King David, to call me queen.

I looked at her with sullen eyes, "I am at the mercy of both God and man. Tell Anushka to return to our home and rest. In seven days, I shall call for her to again wait on me. First, I need permission from the king for I have been told that he despises foreign slaves in his personal quarters."

I was grateful for the mint tea and even more grateful that Eliana and Anushka were friends, so she knew exactly what I needed and why. The hot liquid soothed my exhausted bones. I took long sips and drank deeply, enjoying the taste and scent of the leaves. Alone again with the king, I sat down on the large red cushion that lay on the floor. I idly took in the sight of a huge rug which lay to my right. Made from lion skin, with the lion's head at the base, it was fearsome to look at as it looked so real.

I did not know the king was watching me until I heard him say, "He only bites in the dark of the night."

At his words, I turned swiftly to see a slight grin on his face.

It was hard to imagine this was the same man who had taken me against my will. He looked different. He sounded different.

What I remembered were red eyes and strong hands that had no compassion and left scars on my thigh and arm. What I saw now was a man who was softer, kinder... different.

I could tell he wanted to engage in conversation, but I felt this was not a real marriage, so I had no interest in talking. This was not a man who cared about me in the slightest; he was merely a man determined to hide his sin. To him, I was nothing. I meant nothing. And I wanted to keep it that way.

The moment he started to undress was the moment I had been dreading. How was I going to give myself to him? I knew I had no choice in the matter, not the first time, and certainly not now. I turned my gaze away as he undressed.

I had already been dressed by Naomi in a light gown that covered very little. When Naomi left, I grabbed my veil and wrapped it tightly around my head and my body. My grip tightened on it as though I felt it could protect me from what was about to happen.

Instead of the king coming to where I sat on the cushion, as I had imagined, he went straight to the bed and lay down. "Bathsheba." His voice summoned me. In obedience, I rose to my feet and walked the short distance to where he now lay. "Ah, your feet did not fail you this time."

I immediately recoiled. This was the first mention he had made of that night. Besides asking about the child, it almost felt like nothing had ever happened between us. I imagined he had forgotten, but these words were like a punch to my stomach. He remembered, and he used this fact to mock me. His expression changed as quickly as mine, almost like he wished he had not spoken the words. I trembled as he pulled me towards him, but not from passion — from fear and anger. Fresh tears came raging from my soul and I immediately snatched the veil to my face to wipe them away.

"Bathsheba," he called.

I did not answer, just sat still next to him waiting for him to do whatever it was he desired to do.

"Bathsheba, look at me," he commanded, his voice strong. My eyes met his and he continued. "My queen, you tremble fiercely at my touch. Your heart is filled with fear. Be at peace, Bathsheba I will never hurt you again. Yes, I was a fool once. I took your body and now, though it is mine to take again, this one thing I want to promise you, I will not take it again unless you give it to me."

His words stunned me to stillness and my sobs dried into silence. What did he just say?

He saw the confusion that filled me and laid his hands against my cheeks. "Be at peace, my queen," he whispered. When he held me, I did not push him away. Neither did I move. I just rested and drank in the musky smell of him. His naked skin next to mine was cold. I, however, was still lightly clothed in the manner of a new bride. He looked at me and tugged at my veil. "You will need to let this, and your garment, lie on the floor. We must lay together till the morning. I swear to the God of Israel, I will do you no harm or take my pleasure. Just lie next to me and remain so until the morning when the slaves attend to us. Only for tonight do you need to do this, so our child will have word of a good report."

It was then that I understood what he meant. The way the slaves meet us in the morning mattered if we were to eventually share the news that I was with child. That night and the next five nights that came, we lay in bed side by side, not doing what a man and wife should. He filled his belly with wine, which stilled his loins, and slept close to me while honouring his word.

When the sixth night came, I was happy the marriage time was almost past, and I could return to my own quarters. By now, I had spoken many words with the king, and he spoke many more. He was a wonderful storyteller and from the moment he realised I enjoyed tales he captured my mind with them. He described every word, leaving nothing out. I heard from his own mouth some of the stories I had heard about him from Uriah. He also shared many I had not heard, tales from his youth. He shared the story of the lion that graced the floor and how he had killed it as a young man. He also shared the story of the bear. Most interesting was the story of his fight with the giant. My days and nights were filled with stories, food, and the constant presence of the king.

I realised I had started to think of him as less of a predator and more of a man. It was on our last night together when an unexpected longing to be touched lovingly by him filled me with shame. Even though a few nights previously, Yahweh had spoken, His words gentle, "*Reach for the king,*" I had not. I could not. I refused to betray Uriah's memory even in his death. In this thing, I disobeyed my God.

Chapter Twenty-Six

My heart still grieved over my uncertain future. I did not know what would happen next. I assumed I would be banished to the far side of the palace and live the way that the other wives and concubines lived, only being summoned for the pleasure of the king when he desired it or, in my case, not at all as he had made a vow to God not to touch me unless I touched him first. I would be useless to the king. I sighed at the thought, not sure if it was one of relief or sorrow.

I reprimanded myself, reminding myself not to look beyond the moment and to keep trusting God. I carried a son that would fill my heart with joy; a son I would be able to raise in the king's palace as a prince, not as a servant. For that, I had only thanks and praise for God. "Praise be to Yahweh," I said, louder than I intended.

At my words, the king turned and smiled: "To what does God deserve praise from your beautiful lips? May His praise never depart from your mouth." He laughed out loud.

"My son. God deserves all the praise for the child that grows within me. He is a gift to wipe away my tears." I said, running my hand over my stomach in a circular motion.

"And how do you know it is a son? Will Yahweh not bless me with a princess? One with skin as soft and eyes as beautiful as yours?" he said, touching my arm in a warm caress and immediately recoiling.

I smiled.

The physical distance in bed did not erase the longing I was sure he wrestled with each night; I had felt the presence of his desire as he drew near in sleep. I watched as he stared at me when he thought I was not looking and, sometimes, I caught myself staring at him too.

"Yahweh has shown me, it is a boy; from the moment I knew of his existence, I just knew in my heart that I carried a son."

Shrugging his shoulders he said, "Another son." He strode to the table which had been laid hours before and grabbed a plate filled with dried fruits. He set it on the cushion next to where I sat and he joined me, urging me to share in his meal.

As I lifted a plump dried fig to my mouth, I sensed an opportunity to lay the request that I had carried for the last six days. "My king," I stuttered. He looked at me, waiting for me to speak. "I have a request from my lord, and I pray that you grant me this one thing," I said, bowing before him.

He placed his hand gently beneath my chin and lifted my head, looking at me in the way he had done for days. This look held a hidden message as though urging me to see his soul. "My queen, ask me anything and I will give it to you as long as

Yahweh has blessed me with it. All the riches in this palace, even my own heart, if you ask it of me, I will give it to you."

I fixed my gaze on his eyes and did not look away. "Tomorrow, as the feast ends, when you escort me to the chambers where you wish me to live the rest of my days, would you permit your servant to bring her maid, an Egyptian slave, a gift from my husband Uriah?" No sooner had the words left my mouth than I wanted to bite my tongue for my mistake.

The king's eyes reddened, and the kindness drained. He flung the fruit in his hand across the room. "I am your husband," he bellowed. "And that..." He pointed towards the chamber that was further down from the room that we had shared these last six days. Although it was not fully part of the King's inner chamber, it was in his living quarters. It gave access to all the communal rooms like the banquet room, the huge bath house and even the king's bed chambers. It stood just a few feet away from the large hall that was the only division. "... that was going to be your chambers. I would not be served by an Egyptian, idol worshipping slave." He spat his words out like weapons filled with fury and venom. I was not certain what annoyed him more deeply, that I referred to Uriah as my husband or that I wanted the comfort of my slave. Something was amiss and I was not brave enough to ask.

I was surprised though, that the king had no intention of sending me far away from him. I had heard that there were women's quarters on the north side of the palace; Naomi had told me that much. In it was a dwelling with a small harem in the middle and it had various large quarters with living rooms and two inner chambers in each. I was told that the quarters were huge and richly furnished; they were designed for the queens to live in luxury but also needed to be well suited to entertain the king. This was where I had thought he would be sending me too. Instead, he had planned to keep me close. Did the king care for me?

Chapter Twenty-Seven

I waited for several hours. In the hope that his anger had dissipated, I went to him. I apologised for speaking out of turn and told him that Anushka worshipped Yahweh. I told him how she threw away all her idols and begged me to teach her about my God. His silence persisted; he looked at me and listened to me but seemed lost in his own thoughts. When he finally spoke, I grasped the cause of his anger.

"I thought after these days, and the time we have spent together, your heart would have softened towards me, to see me as your husband and not just your king. But now I know it is still bound to the dead." He spat out those last words and I could see a vein throb in his temple. "You may welcome your slave in your chambers in the women's quarters." I saw the weight of disappointment on his shoulders as he walked away. That night, I slept alone in the huge bed. I was saddened because it was the night I had believed I would obey that quiet voice that said reach out to him. I would have, not out of love, but more out of duty. But he did not come to me and I did not go to him.

I tossed and turned as anger and sadness battled within me. Did he really think years of love for Uriah would be buried in only a few days? That my heart could be so easily bought with the riches of the palace food, his overpowering presence, and laughter-filled stories?

"Forgive him."

I turned and looked around like a fool, knowing no one was there: it was Yahweh who whispered. I tossed a cushion aside, frustrated. "Why does this burden always fall on me? No, I will not forgive him. I will honour him, I will respect him for I have no choice, but I cannot forgive him, Adonai. He has caused me so much sorrow and my heart bleeds." Fresh tears poured from my eyes and flowed down my face. It felt like they came from the depths of my soul as I cried out in despair. Holding on to the pain and the memories was what kept me going and kept me breathing. It was what kept me honouring Uriah.

"No, my child, it keeps you captive. Forgive him." I heard Yahweh whisper again.

This time, I did not even bother to speak, I just kept shaking my head in defiance.

"Bathsheba, give your pain to me and release him. Forgiveness is not for his sake; it is for yours. Forgive him."

I tossed and turned, unable to settle, unable to rest. My heart squeezed causing physical pain and I longed for relief. I was angry, I could taste it. I could feel it like an almost palpable presence in the room. "Where were you that night, Adonai? Why did you not stop him? Where were you when Uriah died? Why did you not help him? Now, you ask me to forgive him. Where were you when I cried out and I asked you to help me that night? I asked you to protect my husband, but you did not.

No! I will not forgive the King." I wailed and shouted not caring if the words carried to the ears of the King.

I am not sure where this fury came from nor the courage to speak to Yahweh. I believe I may have said even more words than that, but these ones I share I remember in great detail. The presence of the Lord was also in the room. I could feel it. I had audience with Yahweh, and I was going to use it, even if He struck me dead.

"Do you hold Me accountable for the sins of man? Bathsheba, I speak to my children and they hear Me, even as you hear Me now. But not all who hear Me obey Me - even as you disobey Me now. I was there with you my child, for I am everywhere. I held you and cried with you. And when the blood of Uriah cried to Me as it spilled on the earth, I lifted his spirit to Myself."

The words burned in my soul; the truth of them stung me. Yahweh spoke to me several nights ago and I did not obey. I chose not to obey and He did not force me. How true his words were. He spoke, it was I who did not listen.

I turned around and looked at the empty room, one side dark and the other lit by candles and scented lamps. I realised at that moment that I no longer needed to look for Yahweh, not in my dreams, not even in a sign such as a firefly. He had revealed Himself to me as Yahweh, the God that is everywhere!

I leapt out of bed and paced the large room, allowing the cool tiled floor to soothe my bare feet. I did not know when it happened, this transition from dreaming to hearing, but somewhere along the way, Yahweh's whispers to my heart settled me. Whether I was praying or not, it seemed like He was constantly speaking, and His words sometimes brought comfort, but most times brought direction that I found hard to follow. I wanted to obey but I did not know how. "How do I forgive him? He has not even asked for my forgiveness. How do I forgive someone who has not requested it? Is he even filled with remorse?" By this time, I was at the window, looking at a starless sky. I could still hear the music; the palace court was still filled with people eating, drinking, and partying. The feast continued. There was joy in their hearts, but sadness filled mine.

And then the Lord whispered words that kept me awake for many hours to come. *"Do you place more value on the words of David or mine? Even if David does not ask you to forgive him, I do. Forgive him, Bathsheba."*

After many sleepless hours, as soul and spirit wrestled, I finally whispered, "I forgive him," and fell into a deep, dreamless sleep.

Chapter Twenty-Eight

The next morning, I woke up tired. I felt like I had wrestled with Yahweh and lost. But I felt something that I had forgotten — peace. It washed over me as quickly as the presence of Yahweh did. By now, the morning was far gone. King David was already fully dressed and at the banquet table. Other mornings, he had worn only a light tunic, his chest pushing against the smooth fabric tight enough for me to see it rise and fall. His long thick hair would fall down the sides of his face as though kissing his cheeks. He looked normal, like every other man, so normal that we would sit and speak and only when he was being served would I remember he was the king.

But this morning, there was no mistaking who he was. He wore a purple cloak, his long hair tied back from his face and tucked firmly under his ornate crown. As I approached the table, I noticed him look at me for an instant and then look back to the large goblet before him. It seemed to be filled with hot liquid rather than wine.

"My lord," I said, bowing before him, waiting for an invitation to sit and eat with him.

"Bathsheba, join me."

I looked up at him in stunned silence, Bathsheba? Just Bathsheba? For the last six days he had called me *"my queen"* and now, I was just Bathsheba.

I am not sure why it hurt me so much but it did. My emotions confused me. I wished I had not forgiven him. I hated the way he seemed to dismiss me, to ignore me. It brought back the painful memories of being used and cast aside without a second glance. I filled my plate with more than I had ever done, thinking filling my heart with food would make it merry. Where was Yahweh now? Why did He not tell the King to forgive in the same way He had told me to? Not that I had done much wrong aside speaking of my late husband Uriah with much fondness as though he still lived. He was indeed my husband, was he not? I felt angered and bothered and continued placing one morsel after another of food into my mouth without chewing or thinking.

"Now I do believe it is a son. Only a strong man in the making would require such a feast."

I raised my gaze to see the king watching me and my cheeks warmed. I could feel the glow radiate into the room.

My mouth was filled with so much food I could not respond, my dilemma was obviously a source of amusement to him as his laughter filled my ears. I held on to my stomach as though to agree with him; yes, let us blame the unborn child for my gluttony and not the confusion in my heart. We continued to eat in silence; this time however I was mindful to only eat what I could chew and swallow quickly in case I needed to speak.

There were moments when I could feel him watching me. I wondered what he was thinking but he did not say, and I was too afraid to ask.

We still had the rest of the day to spend together; it was not until the sun was setting that I would be escorted from his chambers. I wondered if he would come with me or leave the task to someone else. I looked beyond the hall and down the corridor to the room he said he had intended for me. It would have been a much shorter walk, but it would have also meant I would have been closer, much closer to him than I wanted to be. Lost in my own thoughts, I hardly noticed when he sat opposite me in the living quarters. I was on the red floor cushion that I had come to love, and he, on a beautiful purple chair with legs of gold with feet in the shape of a lion's head.

"Will you be taking that red cushion with you? It seems to know you much better than I." He lifted his cup to his lips. This time, it was wine that spilled from the corner of his mouth and trickled down his chin.

"If my husband, the king permits, yes, it will give me much pleasure to take with me something that is yours to cherish." As the words came out of my mouth, I cringed inside. I was trying to make things right and from the look on his face, I was failing. He just stared beyond me, not directly at me, saying nothing. He raised the goblet to his lips once more.

The long silence was uncomfortable; this last day began to mirror the first. I was not sure what seven days with the king would be like. I had little time to think or prepare but even in the short time that I had, nothing I had imagined compared to what had actually happened. It made me question the value of anxiety and worry which truly served no purpose.

There was so much I wanted to say, so much more I wanted to ask him. There were some stories he had left unfinished, but more importantly one question burned in my heart, and I needed an answer. Why did he redeem me?

"Bathsheba, there is so much more that you could have had besides the red cushion, but if that is only what your heart desires, then take it with my blessing."

I could see the way he clenched his fist around the gold cup that was again filled with honeyed wine.

I could not understand the king. Why was he so angry with me? The question rested at the tip of my tongue; fear pushed it back. Wisdom held me grounded. I hated not having the freedom to speak. With Uriah, I could always say my mind, anytime I wanted. There was no protocol between us. This was all new to me, most times, I did not know what I was supposed to be doing — when to bow or not to bow, to smile or not to smile, to sit or stand. All these things I did not know. Nothing in my life had prepared me for life in the palace. I was so thankful; I would soon be cast aside to the far corner of the palace and there, nothing would be required of me as a queen. I was only one of his eight wives: there were others more suited than me.

Later that afternoon, the King was in the living quarters playing his harp quietly, looking out one of the windows towards the city square. I had been reluctant to rise from his presence because the music soothed me. But as time moved on it welcomed the presence of Naomi and the other slave girls, a reminder that my time with the King had come to an end. I listened as they placed my items in large baskets. I heard the water fill the basin and a few moments later, the tap on my shoulder from Naomi requesting my presence in the inner room.

As I was being dressed, I overhead two of the slave girls speaking out of turn. "The king has requested three concubines tonight. Did his new wife not please him at all?" One laughed.

"If it were me, he would be so drained; he would be unable to walk," the other responded.

Their laughter found its way from the bath house to the dressing room where Naomi now brushed my hair.

I looked at the mirror. My cheeks flamed red as embarrassment flooded through my entire body. Is this the rumour that would be spread about me — the woman unable to please the king? I am not sure why this troubled me so much, but it did. I was angry. Men could be careless about matters of the heart, having no loyalty to love, but women? I expected them to understand these things. My husband's body was barely cold. Did nobody care? Naomi placed two pins to hold my short hair in place and put my crown back on.

"My queen, your beauty leaves even the pagan gods speechless," she said, perhaps to cheer me up. She stained my cheeks with red paint as well as my lips; she lined my eyes with dark blue kohl and put perfume behind my ears as well as at the tips of my hair and on each side of my wrists. "The king will miss your presence as will I. I am not called to serve at the women's quarters, but I know I will see you in the king's chambers again soon."

I smiled at her kind words. I would miss her.

These last six days she had served the king and I dutifully, always seeming to appear at just the right time. There were times I wondered whether she watched us through a hidden wall as she always arrived at the right moment to clear the dishes, or to draw a bath. It seemed like she materialised out of nowhere just when needed.

"Thank you, Naomi, you have indeed been kind and I too will miss you. I don't expect to be called anytime soon, but when I am, I hope to see your face."

She smiled as she placed my veil over my head, the last bit of clothing before I was finally dressed and ready to leave. All my bags had been packed overnight, a place had been prepared in the women's quarters and I had been told by Eliana that Anushka was already waiting for me. The king had sent for her only moments after we had spoken and several slaves had a sleep-deprived night as they built a new bed and prepared a new wing, adjacent to the Harem, for me. This served as a reminder that the king had truly not planned to send me there at all, making my heart ache.

"I will see you soon, my queen. You wait and see," Naomi insisted.

My curiosity bubbled over so I asked, "How can you be so sure?"

She frowned in deep contemplation and then she smiled sweetly. "I have served the king for the last ten years and in all this time, never have I heard the king laugh the way he laughs when he is with you. Nor have I seen him stare at any of the queens the way he stares at you." Placing her hand firmly on my shoulder, she bowed close to me and whispered, "The king will call for you."

Chapter Twenty-Nine

When the time came for me to leave, the king placed his harp to one side and walked towards me. As he approached me, I heard the pitter patter of scurrying feet as the room emptied. Alone, perhaps for the last time, I watched him watching me. His eyes scanned the length and breadth of me, drinking me in like I was served in a wine cup.

"Your gifts have gone ahead of you, but this one, I wanted to give to you myself." He reached into his robe past the cloak and into his tunic. In his right hand was a cloth and with his left, he pulled me closer to him as he lowered himself on to a red chair, causing me to sit beside him. Then, he gently unwrapped the cloth.

In his palm was a beautiful gold chain with two doves as a pendant. They sat so close together it almost looked like a heart. It was delicately woven, gold intertwined with coloured stones that I had never seen before. It was beautiful. My eyes moved from his palm to his face; the softness in his eyes troubled me. When he picked up the necklace in both hands, I turned away from him, and took in a sharp breath as his hand gently brushed my hair away from my neck, giving room for him to place the chain around my neck. The cool metal touching my skin made me shiver and the King rested his palm on my back as though to warm me.

My hand immediately went to my chest, touching the birds — birds which had come to mean more to me since that first vision from Yahweh. The king did not know of my dream, as it was not one of the stories I had told. As I held the precious gift, it felt like it was more from my God than my husband, a simple reminder that indeed Yahweh was everywhere. That was the only explanation I could find. The same God who spoke to me, spoke to the king as well. "I serve the God who is everywhere," I whispered, causing King David to lean closer.

I was incensed by his tenderness: was he so quick to forget? I was also incensed by my own weakness. The way my skin responded to his touch invoked within a sense of betrayal, and guilt rushed in. I turned around to look at him, wrestling with all the emotions that tumbled inside me, fear the most prominent of them all. I remembered the day I heard of Uriah's death. My biggest regret was not having the courage to approach him, to go and speak to him. Again, I was faced with a dilemma, what if this was the last time I would see the king? Without further thought, my mouth spoke before my brain could stop the words.

"Why did you marry me? Was it because you defiled me?"

Immediately, he flinched and raised his hand.

My hands flew to my face as I expected him to strike me. He was not Uriah who had made a promise to protect me and to be tender to me. But I did not feel the weight of the king's fist. Instead, he moved my hands away and turned my face towards him. I could see the moisture in his eyes, but it only seemed to settle in the corner. I closed my eyes, refusing to meet his gaze. I always knew my mouth would be the death of me. In that moment, I was too focused on my own needs that I forgot the need to keep my child alive. I am not sure what I was expecting to hear; it did not matter why he married me.

There were so many people who had told me I should be grateful I was chosen by the King. From my Saba to my aunty, to Anushka and even Naomi, they called me blessed. I knew that there were many women, both free and slave who would fall at the feet of the King without question. The same ones who considered me lucky. I did not feel lucky or blessed. I felt betrayed, I felt used, I felt angry because of the truth — my feelings did not matter. I had no choice. But he did, he was the king. He had a choice and he chose me. Why?

When his hands left my face, I opened my eyes as they moved to my stomach. This was the first time the king had ever touched me there. His hands lingered on my stomach as if that was his answer. I let out a deep sigh: it was his child he cared for, and he married me to protect his child. I was relieved but a small part of me was disappointed.

"I married you because I wanted to make you mine." His voice lingered and he paused on the last word. He lifted his hand from my stomach to my face. "That is why I married you, my queen. Not just for the sake of this seed." He rose to his feet, his forehead creased as though he was in deep contemplation.

I sensed there was more to be said, so I waited, placing my hands on my stomach where his had just been.

"At first, my loins controlled me, and then, my heart betrayed me and alone I share the burden of my emotions as yours are..."

he stopped, as though his last words were heavy. "...Yours are far from me." This sounded like pain and regret.

My throat felt dry, the realisation of his words was heavy. The king cared for me. Did he love me? He did not say more, he looked at me once more, touched my face tenderly, turned his back to me and walked away.

Chapter Thirty

I t turned out that Naomi was wrong, and I was right. The king did not call for me. Not even after word was sent to him, exactly four weeks after the last time that I saw him, that I carried his child. That night, the bells of celebration filled the palace and the king had a feast with his counsel and friends. I heard how elaborate it was and I also heard from Eliana, who now brought word straight to me, that the King danced and praised Yahweh the whole night for blessing him with a new wife and a new child. "Joy filled his bones," she said. But even then, he still did not call for me.

Many months came and went, and the baby grew stronger each day. I spent most of my days in the company of women; doing anything I could to keep busy. There was not a lot I was required to do. There were so many servant girls around me that I had no need to even feed myself if I chose not to. The life of a queen was not without luxury but it was lonely. I felt so lonely even in the midst of the crowd of people that flocked in and out of the chambers, with or without my invitation. I was grateful to have Anushka with me; she became more like a sister and less of a slave. There were many other people to do the chores that she would normally do, so she only focused on my personal care.

Although I did not see the King, I heard from him constantly. Not a week passed without gifts from him; sometimes, more than once in a week. I had more fabric and gold than I could count and the rich food started to expand more than just my stomach.

One day, as the evening started to turn into darkness, Anushka tossed aside the bedding like she usually would, inviting me to rest. I reluctantly stood from the red cushion and went to settle myself in the large bed, tossing aside two soft feather pillows that were the newest gifts from the king. Anushka did not leave my bed chamber. Instead, she pulled the small wooden bench near my bedside and sat on it. I was grateful that I would finally be told the reason for the sullen face she had carried all week.

"I have waited longer than usual for your words, share them and tell me what bothers you," I prompted her after she sat in silence much longer than was needed.

"I worry for the birth, my queen."

I frowned at her words, worry? Why would she be worried?

There was still two months till the baby was to be born and if Yahweh wills, perhaps the baby will be delayed beyond the usual time. "Yahweh Himself will help me; can you not see His hand in this matter?" I said placing my hand on my necklace to remind myself of both the Lord and my husband. The first time Anushka saw my crown and necklace, she bowed down and cried to Yahweh for many hours. Where had her faith gone now?

"No, my queen, you misunderstand me. When a woman is with child, her body becomes a sweet scent to her husband and his to hers, especially during the last months. This causes her to lay frequently with her husband as it makes for an easier birth".

There are things you hear that make you thankful that you heard them. This was one of those things. The last few weeks, my dreams had been filled with unspeakable things and my body had burned with desire in a way I thought a woman should not crave. Could it be the way of nature? Was it the child within me that caused me to hunger for the touch of a man? I weighed Anushka's words as her wisdom ushered in my understanding.

"I had hoped the king would call for you. Each night, I have prayed. Was all not well at the seven days of feasting?"

Although I had told her much about what we shared, especially recounting the stories he told, there were some things that felt too personal, too private to share.

I allowed silence to hover between us for a while until, finally, I opened my mouth to tell her the truth. "I did not lay with the king as a woman should. He said he would not force me again and he would only touch me if I touched him first." I did my best to summarise his words. "I did not touch him, I could not. My heart was grieving for Uriah. My body belongs to Uriah. How could I give it to the King of my own free will? It was his to take, he did not take it, and I would not give it." It had been many months since I had cried, but that day, I sobbed like a child. I did not even know why I was crying, but there was a heaviness that I had been carrying. Anushka held on to me and sang. I closed my eyes until she believed I was asleep and left me, closing my inner chamber door firmly behind her. Alone, I opened my eyes, sat up in the dark room, and prayed.

I had prayed constantly for the last few months, much more in the last few weeks as a weight I did not understand seemed to hang over me. Each time I would pray for relief and each time Yahweh would say, *"Give it to me Bathsheba."* But I did not know what the 'it' was supposed to be. What was this burden that I carried that weighed so heavily on my heart?

"Yahweh, take it, please take it from me. It is too heavy. I am so weary, please take it away." I cried out from the depths of my soul.

"Forgive him, Bathsheba, and let him go."

As I heard the voice of the Lord, I wept louder, and confusion ran through my bones. I had forgiven King David, I spoke the words out, what else was there to forgive?

My heart, body and mind welcomed sleep that night and I dreamt for the first time in so long. In my dream, I was walking towards the market square, not the central market but the much smaller one that was on the other side of Jerusalem, only a short distance from Mount Moriah. It was to this market that foreign traders brought the more expensive items for sale. In the distance, I could see Uriah, his hands and feet were bound with ropes like a slave waiting to be sold. I ran to him wanting to go and free him. My waist pouch was filled with coins, I was going to buy him back for myself. My feet felt slow but picked up speed as I approached him, then I saw some other women and two men all running towards him. It seemed they too wanted to purchase him.

When I finally got to him, I struggled to breathe and allowed my heart to rest now that my feet had stopped. "I want to buy him," I screamed, watching with joy as I saw Uriah's face turn towards mine. He seemed to say something, but I was not listening to him: there would be more time for talking later. For now, I needed to get him back home. I looked up at the trader throwing him all I had in the pouch; I did not even bother to count it. When the merchant turned towards me, my mouth fell open as I stared at my own reflection. I looked from the merchant to Uriah.

There were tears flowing down his face. His words were loud and clear. "Let me go, Bathsheba."

I held my ears and began to scream "Noooooooooooooooooooooooo." The noise echoed and was fit to wake both the living and the dead.

I opened my eyes as Anushka shook me awake. I tried to re-adjust to the darkness around me. I pushed her away, climbing out of my bed and on to my knees. She hesitated for a moment and then again, she walked out of the door.

The Lord kept speaking:

"Forgive him, Bathsheba, and let him go."

This time, I understood the words of Yahweh. It was not King David I had to forgive; it was Uriah.

"Why did you not just come home to me?" I spoke like he could hear me. The bitter taste of disappointment and anger overwhelmed me. If only he had come home to me, he would still be with me. Why did he not just come home? I could never forgive him; I would never let him go.

I turned my face as though away from God, but as I did, I remembered how pointless it was. God was everywhere. To my left or to my right, in front or behind, He was there.

"I know you are filled with sorrow and your heart bleeds, but if you give it to Me, I will repay you with much more than you have lost. Forgive him, Bathsheba, and let Uriah go."

I learned that night that bitterness was a choice. It was only when I gave Uriah into the hands of God that the pain that had settled in my back, in my feet and many nights in my head, seemed to disappear. My heartbeat slowed to a peaceful rhythm and my breathing calmed. It seemed like for all those months, I had stopped breathing. The relief was slow but steady and over the next few weeks, I kept praying through the pain. Each day, I let go just a bit more. Forgiving Uriah was much harder than forgiving King David. At first, I did not understand why. I turned to Anushka for advice instead of keeping the emotions locked inside my head, and my heart. I was grateful for her confidence, to share my thoughts and feelings with her. It was she who upon several days of quiet reflection showed me the piece of the puzzle that put my heart at rest.

With her words, I was able to understand that when the King defiled me, he had no loyalty to me; he just took what he wanted. Like many other men who defiled women. It was not right, it was unjust, but it was the way with some men. They were controlled by their own lusts and passions. However, with Uriah, my husband, bound to me before man and God, I felt a deep sense of betrayal. He chose to honour the King more than he chose to honour me. His duty to the Crown, to his soldiers, to a nation that was not even his, was much stronger than his love for me. It was that rejection that cut so deeply, almost to my very soul. The thing I loved most about him was the thing I came to hate in the end. He was a man of war; he was a man of honour. It made no sense to me, the blind loyalty he had to the man who had betrayed him with his own wife. But it was time for me to accept it, to forgive and let go.

The sun shone through the windows, brightening not only the room but my heart. The colours seemed more vibrant and almost danced before my eyes. Sweet smells entered my chambers through the open windows. Peace swept across me. It may not last. But in that moment, I felt almost happy.

"You think Yahweh dealt wickedly towards you, but, my queen, do you not think that death can also be a type of kindness? Uriah died loving you; he was spared from the pain of the truth. He died with peace, doing what he was born to do. Had he been alive, would you not have killed him with the truth? I have come to know you so well since the first day I served you; I know that your mouth would not have kept quiet to the truth of this child."

I knew she was right. My words would have killed Uriah.

As I had expected, the realisation did not erase the pain, and time had not done that either, but Yahweh worked on my heart as I cried out my pain, my shame, my guilt. With time, the grief became lighter and my heart became softer.

Chapter Thirty-One

When the eighth month came, it felt like my son was at war inside me. It seemed like I carried a warrior. His constant movement kept me both amused and awake. Beside me was another basket of gifts from my elusive husband. I pondered on Naomi's words again. It had been six months since I had been alone with the King. I had seen him many times, at the banquets he held at various occasions as well as the Sabbath meals. At those times, he stayed far from me, so I could not touch him or hold his gaze, though a part of me longed for it. But he was close enough for me to enjoy the strong scent of him, one that I had known so well in those seven days we spent together. The scented oil rubbed into his skin was made not just from flowers, but also from wood. It was strong, yet sweet. Crafted by foreign hands, brought to Jerusalem by merchants, only worn by the King.

I joined the women to prepare the evening meal and I decided to bake raisin cakes. I let my mind wander and settle on different thoughts. I kneaded the dough harder, as though I could somehow transfer my mixed emotions into it. I had taken to baking bread, cakes and sewing fabrics with the slaves. It was a way to pass time. At first, it displeased them to be in the company of their queen, as it meant they were quiet in their labour, but as time passed, they eased into my company, and I heard the tales of their lives. Some were more colourful than others, and some shared details that a godly woman should not recount. I heard in much detail, the way some of these women lay with men with little more skill than the temple prostitutes. It shocked me at the ease with which they recounted private matters, yet, I listened in silence.

My movement was no longer like it was just a few months before as the weight of the baby settled and caused my back to ache. I found some relief in Anushka's tiny but firm hands, massaging hot oil into my back, but the pain persisted most days. Out of nowhere, a deep longing for the king warmed me and filled my soul. I remembered the tenderness of his skin on mine as his hand lingered on my neck and then the top of my back. I remembered the day he placed the necklace on me. The touch that felt unwelcome months ago, I am ashamed to say, I now craved deeply. I remembered Anushka's words and heat flooded over me. It was the baby; my mind was unsettled because of the baby. These feelings, these unexpected long-ings, yes, it was the baby. That was a much easier truth to accept.

As I worked my way through the dough, trying my best to ignore the kicking and turning of my little warrior, a thought formed. I am not sure if it was mine or a whisper from God, but suddenly, I knew exactly what I was going to do. I carefully shaped the raisin cakes into small portions and passed it to Anushka to place in the coal. As soon as they were cooked, I picked up a fresh basket, placed two soft white linen cloths on it, and then I lifted six hot raisin cakes — the biggest, softest, and thus most tasty ones — and covered them. I pressed the basket in Anushka's hands. "Find Eliana and give this to her. Ask her to take it to the king at once. Bid her to say — this has been made for the king by the hands of Bathsheba." Immediately, she took the basket and left my presence. I looked outside, it was late evening, and the sun was now resting. I prayed that my gift would be a welcome treat, something sweet for the king to enjoy just before he laid down to sleep, a perfect accompaniment to the wine he loved to drink.

Two would have been enough, the cakes were a good size, but I considered that he might be entertaining guests. I frowned at the thought, but instead of dwelling on it, I turned my face aside and prayed, "Yahweh, please, let him accept my gift."

It was not news in the palace that I had not spent time alone with the King; I had felt the weight of judgment and speculation for months. I acted like it did not bother me, though I had hoped that the King would consider me and call me to hide my shame. The same way he had planned we would lay side by side unclothed the first night, that was the same way I had hoped he would at least summon my presence, even if just once. Surely, he would have heard the whispers.

Each time Saba visited me, he asked me the question I dreaded. "Have you been with your king?"

Each time, I shook my head and nothing more was spoken on the matter. I wondered why my Saba did not ask the King the same question. But I knew the answer, he was not at liberty to discuss the King's private matters with him. Men were not like women who shared such details.

"All is well, my child; we can already see the fruit of your union," he would say loudly, breaming with pride and pointing at my stomach. I was so thankful that I carried the king's child. It lessened the weight of the careless words spoken in and outside the palace.

From my Saba, I heard news of my father's injury and recovery at war. I heard that he fared well, and he also sent word of his gratitude to the king. He took pride in not only being one of the King's Thirty, but also being the father of the queen. I smiled as I remembered fondly my Saba's last visit.

Anushka arrived much quicker than I had anticipated. The palace was huge. I was in the far corner of the north wing and from the last I heard, the king was in the west. Although he had a chamber in every part of the palace, his main residence was in the west wing, high above the banquet hall, only a short distance from the courts of men and his throne room. It was there I had spent those seven days with him. I later learned that I was the first and only wife the king had even taken into his private residence for his seven days of feasting.

"Did you run?" I asked Anushka. "How have you returned so soon?" I regarded her, taking in her appearance.

She seemed calm, not looking to catch her breath. "Eliana was coming to me as I was going to her. She was dismissed for the night; the King had retired to his inner chambers early to rest."

I looked at her empty hands. "Where are the raisin cakes? Did you set them down before you came to me?"

She shook her head and smiled. "No, my queen. I insisted to Eliana that she must take them to the king. Though she refused and pleaded for her head, I insisted she must go, and pleaded for mine. Tonight, wisdom won, and you did what no one has done previously. Your courage must not go without purpose. The king is in his north chambers. I hear that for the last week, Queen Abigail was taken with a strong fever, and he had visited her".

I trembled at her words. The King was so close? My heart beat faster and hammered inside my chest. This was much sooner than I expected. I did not think the word would come so soon, but if he was only a short distance away, Eliana would either return with a message or be dead by the morning. I had hoped that my gift would have gone along with his other meals or with a jug of wine. How could I know that he would dismiss the slaves this early in the day? And why? Was the king sick as well? Or perhaps he was with company. None of that seemed to hold my attention for long as I focused on praying for Eliana. I prayed fervently for her soul. How foolish I had been. As she was one of the King's food bearers, I hoped she would fare well as I did not want her blood on my hands. That sweet girl did not deserve such a fate.

As I closed my eyes and wrestled with my decision trying to pray, Anushka tapped my shoulder. I looked up and saw Eliana walk in. My heart sank as in her hands was the basket, still covered, exactly as I had given it to Anushka. I heard a few giggles as she walked the length of the room towards me.

Chapter Thirty-Two

Anushka quickly hushed them and dismissed them to their chores. I prayed the ground would open and swallow me. I had become the object of laughter. Was death not better than the life I was living?

The king's rejection cut deep. I wondered why my gift was so unacceptable to him. Even if he did not want to eat it, why did he not throw it to the wild dogs? And as for Eliana, I was thankful she was alive, but rage rose within me and, for once, I was going to assert my position as a queen. How dare she bring disgrace into my chambers? Did she not have the better judgement to throw the basket away? Will she dare to come and mock me before my slaves?

Anushka, sensing my anger, rose to her feet before I rose to mine. I was unstable and staggered. She caught me and held me as I wept. By this time, Eliana had reached us. "Did you see the king and set the meal before him?" I heard Anushka ask. It was a sensible question. Perhaps she was not granted audience by the king's soldiers; maybe the king was already asleep.

"I set it before the King." Eliana responded and immediately, my heart sank. His rejection was confirmed. A life of solitude flashed before my eyes like a living nightmare. I grabbed on to my stomach, my son, previously asleep, now tumbled in my womb. I rubbed my belly gently to calm him, I had learnt that my mood affected him, and I wanted him to be at peace even if I was not.

"Set it aside, Eliana, and leave us. You have no need to do more tonight." I was glad Anushka took charge as I could utter no words. I let the tears flow, not caring who watched. Maybe they will learn something from my grief, even if the only lesson was the unfairness of life.

"No, my lady, the king sends words for the ears of the queen, please let me speak."

I looked at Eliana. A smile twitched at the corners of her lips. Did she mock me? Was she blind to my distress?

"Speak freely before Anushka, her ears are as good as mine."

Eliana looked from me to her friend and back to me. "My king said, Eliana, go and tell my queen that the hands that baked this cake should be the hands to bring them and feed it to me tonight."

I blinked repeatedly as joy rushed through my veins.

Anushka immediately jumped to her feet and started barking instructions to various girls. "Fill the basin."

"Heat the rose oil and add in some honey."

"Bring a fresh gown."

A flurry of movement ensued and a few brief hours later I was cleansed from head to toe and dressed in a long red gown. It had been brought to my chambers only a few days ago in a basket of fabric and jewellery, another gift from the King. I loved it the minute I laid eyes on it. Soft to the touch, the neck was cut low and adorned with white stones. When I was first dressed in it, I was disappointed; it was too tight around the waist. I had told Anushka to keep it until the baby was born, but she had insisted on taking out the stitches at the sides. She added some gold fabric to the waist, giving it the extra width that was needed.

"When the baby is born, I can always unstitch the extra fabric, but for now, enjoy the beauty of it. A soft gown is one of life's little pleasures which must not be put aside."

I am so glad she did. Although I had many other gowns, the red one felt befitting for the night. It was perfect. The colour matched the colour of my lips that had been stained with red paint. My eyes were darkened, but my cheeks left bare. My hair had grown just below my shoulders. Anushka had braided it and pinned it to the top of my head for months, but that night, she unpinned it and washed it, then she brushed it straight with hot oil causing it to glisten. It fell freely around me. Finally, she placed my crown on my head. When I stepped into the red gown, it fit perfectly; there was enough room for my baby to kick and more for me to breathe. The silk settled on my skin, cooling me and making me feel radiant.

I smiled as I looked at my reflection in the long mirror. I was beautiful. I was ready to go and feed my husband and my king. Excitement moved my tired legs, and I forgot the pain in my back as I walked with Eliana out of my chambers. As I approached the door, Anushka whispered, "Yahweh goes before you, my queen. Let the dead rest with their maker and the living serve the purposes of Yahweh."

I knew what her words meant. I smiled as I walked outside the door not looking back. This time, the whispered words were different; I held my head high, walking boldly to my husband's chambers.

Chapter Thirty-Three

There were three guards in front of me; Eliana stood just behind them. Two more slaves from my own chambers also stood in front of me, with two behind me, and six soldiers behind them. If you had seen the procession, you would have thought I was being escorted from one nation to another rather than between chambers.

I often wondered why there were so many guards. The life in the palace lacked any privacy. Even in the bath house, there was always someone there, drawing the water, cleansing my skin. The only time I had any shred of privacy was when I was asleep; even then, there was always a slave outside my bed chamber. I was never alone, except when I went and relieved myself of my body's waste. I absolutely refused to let anyone wash my private areas like I was a child. I shivered at the thought. I cherished those moments of solitude and enjoyed the privacy but not as much these last few months as the smell from my own waste scared me. I heard it was so for a woman with child; the frequency increased and the smell of what was expelled worsened.

I was so deep in thought that I lost focus of my surroundings, until we approached the king's door. I suddenly recognised where I was and recoiled. This was the same chamber I had been in all those months ago. The one I was snuck into like a thief in the cover of night. "Oh Adonai, why has he brought me here again?" My pace slowed and bitterness filled my mouth as fear gripped me and heat flashed up my back. Panic filled my bones, and my legs began to wobble.

Three loud knocks later, the main chamber doors opened before us. As the procession walked in, my head swayed and I could hear loud thudding in my ears, "Please, Yahweh. Please." I prayed under my breath knowing that I was not okay. My hands were wet; I rubbed them against my dress. I pulled my veil lower, trying to hide my fear and forced my feet to move one in front of the other. One step at a time. I only had to focus on one step at a time. Unfortunately, my left foot got caught in the corner of the rug, and I tripped. Just before I lost my balance, I felt the weight of my slave girls grab me before I hit the ground. Their groans as they took my weight hung in the otherwise silent room.

Eliana rushed to my side, grabbing the basket from my hands, ignoring a few of the cakes that had now spilled out to the floor. "My queen" was all she said.

I opened my eyes. I had tripped but not fallen, saved by the slaves behind me. Now, I was grateful for their presence. Sometimes the enemy was not a person, it was a thing. I chuckled at the thought and tried to pick up what dignity I had left. This was not the entrance I had hoped for. I realised that shame was a stronger emotion than fear or anger for what bothered me most in that moment was no longer the chambers; it was the misfortune of appearing like a fool before the king. My cheeks were burning. I held my head low.

"Take that thing out of here," I heard as one of the King's guards screamed the order, pointing at the offending rug.

"Place her in the inner room and call the physician at once." This time, it was the king who spoke, and the room was suddenly filled with a flurry of movement. I felt a twinge in my side and instinctively I rubbed my stomach to ease the pain. Eliana followed the four girls who carried me; she placed the basket of raisin cakes on the silver tray next to the kings' jug. "Leave us until the physician arrives."

The room immediately emptied, and I was alone with him. I swallowed and tried to sit up on the bed, but he held me down.

"Rest for a moment," he said quietly. When he brought his cup to my lips, I drank deeply. The wine was sweet and strong and I closed my eyes to savour its taste. The memory of our first night came without invitation; I wiped my mouth as I tried to push it away.

I looked at the floor, remembering how I had crawled there, then at the bed and finally at him. His eyes briefly met mine and then he looked away. I wondered if he even remembered that night. Three sharp knocks echoed through the chamber, breaking the moment.

"Enter," the king commanded, and the guards opened the huge door to a small man with two women in tow. For the next few minutes, I was prodded from head to foot. Then, one of the women placed her cold hand on my stomach, pressing it. It did not hurt but discomfort meant I gasped. She then placed her left ear on my exposed stomach, tossing my red gown aside.

When the baby kicked her head, she quickly moved and smiled. "He has the strength of the king," she whispered.

She welcomed back the small man who examined my eyes, my mouth, my ears and felt my inner wrists. "Do you feel fine within, my queen?" he asked.

I nodded my head and recounted the story, assuring him that I did not actually hit the ground. They spoke with the king for a few minutes and then walked swiftly through the door.

Alone with my husband, I no longer needed my veil, so I uncovered my head and put it to one side. I looked at the king who still had his back turned to me. There was so much I wanted to say. My heart was heavy. I hated this room and this bed. I struggled from the bed, my pregnancy making me ungainly, removed my cloak, then walked towards a long bench. It was covered with fine sheep's wool, woven into a soft fabric to give comfort. King David lifted the basket of cakes and walked towards me. He placed it between us and sat on the other side. His eyes downcast, he did not smile or frown. Rather, his face held a blank expression. I did not know what to say, or rather how to say what I wanted to say. Instead, I picked up the pendant and held it between my forefinger and my thumb.

"Your hands baked these cakes for me?" he asked, as though trying to break the silence. I shifted where I sat, kicked in the stomach by my own son. I felt the whole night was ruined even before it started. I was prepared to enjoy his company, to feed him and even to give myself to him, but I was not prepared to be in this room to do it. I looked around me, trying to keep my face away from him, hiding the tears that now flowed.

I felt him move closer and then he touched my hand, gently, "Bathsheba, look at me," he urged. When I turned towards him, there were tears in his eyes and our eyes locked. In that moment, I knew that he remembered. He pulled me towards him, and I wept into his shoulder. His hands brushed my hair softly. "Forgive me, my queen," he whispered. His words broke me, and I cried out, the pain almost physical.

We stayed like that for a long moment; he allowed me to cry out my pain on to his shoulder as he sat quietly and took the brunt of the silent angry words. I wanted to scream but dared not. I only managed to raise my tiny fists and hit his chest repeatedly and I sobbed loudly through unspoken words. When the left side of his tunic was soaked with my tears, he lifted my head carefully and placed it on the right side.

Once I had cried and emptied my soul, my breathing eased and I settled. My head hurt and my eyes stung, but my heart was light. I lifted myself from him, head still low, with both my hands in his. He touched my cheek, and then lifted my chin to turn my face towards his. I looked at him as he looked at me. "Will you feed me, Bathsheba?" he asked tenderly, and I nodded. He moved my unruly hair away from my face, wiping the last tears from my eyes and cheeks and then brushing his fingers across my lips. I shivered at his touch and then he drew me into his arms. I stayed there for a moment, then gently, I raised my hands to his face and touched his chest, my touch tender. He smiled.

Chapter Thirty-Four

It was time to eat; it was time to turn to the purpose for which I came to his chamber. I picked up the basket, broke a piece of cake and raised it to his lips. He opened them gently and took my fingers as well as the cake into his mouth. A warm sensation radiated through my body and the baby moved. I chuckled. Taking the king's right hand, I placed it on my stomach and his eyes widened as he felt his son kick. The king pushed the basket of cakes aside. He lifted my gown and placed both his hands on my stomach and laughed with delight as his son responded to his touch. He brought his lips to my stomach, kissing his child and speaking quiet words that I imagined were prayers to Yahweh. My heart was filled with joy. It amazed me how two strong emotions could co-exist in the same place at the same time. The same heart that was bitter towards the king only a few moments ago was the same heart that welcomed his touch with love. I revelled in his touch as his hands and lips moved over my stomach as though he was connecting in some primal manner with his son.

Without thinking, I placed my hand on the King's head, running my fingers through his hair. It was so soft to touch. It was not until he immediately stopped kissing stomach and jerked his head away that I realised my folly. I watched in shock as different emotions flashed through his eyes and his face reddened. My head felt heavy and I swallowed hard. I had touched the head of the king. No one, except God's prophet or the crown bearer could touch the head of the king; not even the slave girls that bathed him. There were many things the king did not do himself, except that one thing. He washed his own head. To touch it was an offence punishable by death. The king's head, anointed by God's prophet himself, was out of reach to any man or woman.

My face fell into my hands and I shook it with disdain. "Oh Bathsheba," I whispered to myself, "Is there no end to your madness?" I tried to push him away so I could lift myself and beg for my son's life. Mine felt lost already, but he would not move.

"My king!"

"My king!"

This was all I managed to say over and over with my face covered. Although it was only moments, it felt like hours before he reached for my hands. I reluctantly gave them to him. I kept my eyes closed out of deference to him, until I felt him kiss them gently. I opened them and let out a breath I did not realise I was holding. He looked at me and smiled, then took my right hand and placed it first on his neck and then gently, on his head, closing his eyes as he pushed my fingers gently through his thick red hair. He smiled, pulled me closer, and whispered, "Only when we are together, my queen, and never speak of it."

A strong wave of emotion rushed through me as the sense of his acceptance overpowered me. I turned my face to him and placed my open lips firmly on his, with his hand still holding mine in his hair.

That night was the first of many love-filled nights in the arms of the king. When we were alone there was nothing between us. His longing was as strong as mine and our bed was filled with intense pleasure. Many nights I left the king both satisfied and surprised. "Where did you learn these things, Bathsheba?" he would ask in wonder and I would tell him the truth: "From the mouths of the temple prostitutes you gifted me as slaves." He laughed as I recounted some of the tales I had heard from their lips.

Our nights were filled with passion, our days with stories and food. As the weeks passed, the pain in my back increased and the King insisted on rubbing hot oil into it himself. He took such care, gentle so as not to cause too much pain, but often getting carried away with the oil, touching places that brought much relief through sheer pleasure. I was so lost in the moments of love and joy that I lost track of time. It appeared that I had not returned to my chambers for more than four weeks.

It was Eliana who brought word from Anushka, reminding me that the ninth month had come. I needed to return to my chambers so we could prepare for the birth. When the king returned from his throne that evening, I brought the matter to his attention. He objected to my absence. He insisted on having his physician and the palace midwives on standby. I tried to plead my case, but his response was firm.

"You will remain with me, my queen. Only the best physician in all of Israel will attend to the birth of my son," he insisted.

I knew that passion clouded his reasoning, so I did not press the matter further. I allowed for him to be well fed and rested. When we moved into the inner chambers and he lay in my arms, just before he drifted into sleep, I begged for his attention. Not with words but with actions. I tossed and turned, kicking his feet, and sighing heavily until I heard him chuckle.

"What troubles you, Bathsheba?"

"Nothing, my king, my heart is rested."

"My bruised feet tell a different story," He responded, pulling me closer.

With his ears firmly turned to me, I started to state my case as carefully and in as much detail as I could.

"My king," I said.

"Your king? I thought I was your love." He teased.

"I need the ears of my King, so he can save my life."

I could not see the expression on his face, the lamp had been turned down low, but I felt his body tense at my words. "Speak freely."

I tried to think of the right words to say, not wanting to bring up delicate matters of the past. "My king, the baby is ready to be born any day now, but it is much sooner in months than my arrival in the palace. Should I have the baby in the hands of the physician and the palace midwives, they will see him fully grown and well developed. When the months are counted, I will be dragged before you a harlot and stoned to death. But if I have the child, in the hands of my Egyptian slave, the one who holds my confidence and has prepared for this day, the word that will come to you is of an infant born sooner than its time, of a child that is alive but weak, one that requires expert care, strapped always to my bosom. Then, my king shall call on the people for prayers. When a month has passed and the child is declared of good health, all will rejoice and praise God for His mercy. My own life will be spared along with his. Then, my love, we shall be reunited."

King David placed his hand on my stomach. The baby, fast asleep, moved only slightly as though to acknowledge his father's touch. "Let it be done according to the way you have said it. Let us remain tonight, in the morning, you may return to your chambers. Send word daily to my ears."

Moving closer to him, I kissed his right ear tenderly, "Your ears will hear, my love." I ran my fingers through his hair, in the way he had come to enjoy, then pulled him towards me and welcomed him, putting sleep aside till the morning.

Chapter Thirty-Five

The next few weeks were filled with much noise and laughter. My quarters had become a popular meeting place. I was unlike the other queens who asserted their authority and treated the slaves as women who should be seen and not heard. I still saw myself as the same woman; my position had changed but my mind remained the same. To everyone else, I was one of the queens and the women bowed in my presence. To me, I was still Bathsheba. I sat with my servants, worked with them, sewed fabric, cooked meals, wove baskets, listened to their many tales and shared some of my wisdom.

I welcomed my friend Salma and the other wives of the King's Thirty. I had feasts in their honour, and we shared stories of the war. I enjoyed some of the benefits of my crown, having access to more wealth than I could have ever dreamed of. I did not crave it for personal gain; instead, I sent gifts to the widows and food to the poor. When I heard from one of my servants that her sister was going to be sold to the temple as a prostitute to pay her father's debt, I bought her instead. I could not save everyone, but this young child, only twelve years of age, barely a woman, I spared from the life of harlotry.

I also sent offerings to the House of the Lord with thanksgiving. My heart was glad; I was at peace with myself and with my king. I cherished the memories of our time together, longing to be reunited again with him, to listen to his wise words, to watch his fingers play with ease the music that warmed my soul and sent the warrior baby to sleep. There were many things I loved about my king, but the one I loved the most was the way he loved Yahweh. His praise was constantly on his lips. Not many words were spoken without the mention of Yahweh. He gave Him glory for every battle won, whether on the field or in his own heart. He spent many hours in the House of the Lord. We shared more than passion; he told me more than stories. He taught me about Yahweh and the works of His hand and my love for both my God and my King strengthened. My prayer to Yahweh was now without ceasing. I had learnt to see His hand in everything and give Him praise.

Only a powerful God could take such pain and turn it into joy.

Only a mighty God can take such hatred and turn it into love.

Only this one true God would I continue to serve all my days.

As busy as I kept myself, time still crawled. I was desperate to meet my child, but he was not in a hurry to appear. I troubled Anushka's ears daily.

"Will the baby come today?" I would ask.

"When will the baby come?"

"Has the time for birth not yet come?"

Over and over until I am sure her ears bled. I thank Yahweh she was patient with me and hid her frustration well.

"Enjoy the moments of waiting as pain lies ahead before the joy of motherhood. Sleep now while your hands are free," she would warn me, shaking her head. "A new baby feeds constantly and will rob you of much sleep, rest now" she would insist, sending me back to my bed.

I was tired of resting. I was ready to be a mother.

The ninth month came and went, and I began to worry. The baby's movement had eased, and he no longer fought battles in my belly. He seemed to sleep more and move less, not responding to my touch. I carried this burden for many days before I picked up the courage to share it with Anushka, "Is the baby well, Anushka? He has quietened within me. I fear for his life."

She pulled my hands into hers with a reassuring nod. "He is well, he is resting before being born. Perhaps, he has found much comfort and we need to encourage him. Come now, let us take a long walk around the palace grounds and bring *him* some discomfort." She rose quickly and sent word to the guards that the queen would be walking.

Chapter Thirty-Six

It was early evening when we stepped outside the palace doors. We walked the length and breadth of the palace walls. I found it hard to move; my feet were now tight in my sandals, but I was encouraged by Anushka's words. I longed to feel the fresh air on my face, but I was covered with a red royal veil. As we walked past the side entrance to the palace courts, I was met with a surprise. I caught a glimpse of the king through the window to his chamber. Bathed in light from the south facing sun, he stood deep in conversation with his elders. I stopped to take in the sight of him. He was dressed in a red robe; his crown was not on his head but tucked firmly under his right arm and he waved his left hand fast as though it spoke its own language. I had not seen him in many weeks, so I stood and stared, not caring that the guards and servants were watching me watch him.

It was one of the pains of being married to a man you had to share, not just with other women but with the whole of Israel. Even if he raised his head and looked outside the window, he would not see me clearly. I was hidden from his sight, and if he did see me, he would not come to me. By now I had learned that duty was more important than love and a woman's place in a man's heart was not first. Still, seeing him made the walk more pleasurable.

I spent the rest of my time praying, speaking the words I had learnt from the king.

"Great is the LORD, and greatly to be praised.
In the city of our God, In His holy mountain.
Beautiful in elevation, the joy of the whole earth,
Is Mount Zion on the sides of the north,
The city of the great King.
God is in her palaces; He is known as her refuge."

Though I did not understand the words at first, the king took his time to explain it to me. He gave glory to our God, recognising Him as the one true King, the great King, the joy of the whole earth, the one who resides in the Holy Mountain of Zion and is worthy of all our praise. "Yahweh, all praise belongs to you, so I give mine to you."

Though the walk was long and tiring, and it caused my son to wrestle within me, nothing happened that day or even the next. On the third day, morning had just broken when I felt a rush of liquid between my legs along with a sharp pain that took my breath away, leaving me unable to scream. Eventually, I called for Anushka, and commotion rapidly filled my quarters. Pain and excitement quickened my pulse and stole my breath. The baby was coming; I had waited for this moment for more than nine months, but I had craved a child for many years. The pain brought tears along with memories. I grieved for Uriah and the children I had prayed we would have. I grieved for the life we shared. God had not taken away my love for him, He had replaced it.

My soul was at war, memories are heightened in moments of pain and the pain lasted for hours, coming and going with only a few moments of rest. I cannot remember who it was that filled my mouth with bitter herbs. It could not have been Anushka as she firmly held my legs and gave me support as I sat over the birthing stool, but it was her voice that commanded me to drink. I was exhausted from pushing with yet no cry of the baby. I wanted to rest, I wanted to sleep. I felt a hand grip my shoulder and turned to see Eliana who bent and whispered into my ears: "The King is in the House of the Lord; he prays for you." Those were the exact words I needed to hear.

As soon as the pangs of childbirth started, I had sent word to the King and now, he was with his King of kings in prayer for me. Fear gripped my heart and sent ice through my veins: what if it was not a boy? Fresh tears sprang, not only from pain but now from worry. Had I really heard Yahweh, was I truly carrying a son?

Just before the child arrived, my body shivered uncontrollably. With one more push, the baby was born, and I collapsed, away from the birthing stool, my body falling to the cold earth. The baby did not cry immediately.

"Bring the hot cloth and fill the basin with water and salt," Anushka shouted.

I tried to raise my head to look at him but had no strength in me. I heard a sharp slap and then the child screamed.

"Eliana!" Anushka yelled. "Send word immediately to the King. Say to him — your son has come months before his time. He is small, but he is strong." She shouted loud enough for her voice to carry towards the outer room and a sudden burst of merriment was heard from my outer chambers. Songs broke out as various voices rejoiced at the news.

My heart eased into a gentle rhythm as the word son hit my ears. After the boy had been scrubbed with salt and tied in white cloth, Anushka placed him at my bosom and he immediately suckled. I thought I knew what love felt like, or even joy, but nothing prepared me for the emotions that ran through my entire being. I laughed like one who was insane. My son! Oh, how I loved him! I held him tightly, wrapping my blanket over him and praising God and whispering words of prayer for him.

He was so beautiful, his freckled face and dark brown hair with red streaks carried the resemblance of the King. My eyes pricked with tears, grateful that I was alive to nurse him and I would be alive to be his mother under the protection of the King. There was no other way I would have lived beyond the seventh day. If this son had been placed in Uriah's arms, one look and he would have known the child was not his. I realised that it would not have mattered if Uriah came home to lay with me when he was summoned. The truth would not have been hidden for long.

I watched my infant son as he settled into sleep. His cheeks were soft to touch and his head was tender and slightly bruised from the birth. Worry creased my head when he winced when I stroked it.

"The salt water will heal it soon enough." Anushka whispered as though she could read my mind.

I had been unaware of her presence until that moment.

"My queen, you will remain with the baby in your inner chambers for weeks. I alone will attend to you, sending word that the early infant is weak and cannot be moved as yet."

I nodded in agreement, guilty at the lengths we were taking to cover the unspoken deed. I was not ungrateful to Yahweh for the life he had given me as I had the love of my King and his son in my arms.

Yet, the tears that flowed were ones of sorrow. I missed the life I had, the freedom I enjoyed, the man that I loved and the children I longed to have with him. I did not thrive on secrecy. I felt like a lifeless instrument that was played without regard, yielding to the chords of the musician but with no soul. Whether it would be a song of sorrow or praise relied on the choice of the musician and not the instrument itself.

Eliana burst into my inner chambers, dancing and carrying with her a heavy basket filled with gifts of silver and gold. "The King rejoices with song and dancing; he has called his elders and a feast is being prepared." She continued to sing and dance, and many others joined us.

I watched in silence as Anushka ushered them in, directing them to the far corner of my inner chambers. I enjoyed the rendition, putting my own thoughts and sorrow aside. What could I change now?

It was a time of great joy. I rejoiced with them for a moment, before Anushka bid them farewell, closing the door firmly behind them. What I did not know at the time was that the rejoicing would be short-lived and death was waiting on the other side.

Chapter Thirty-Seven

The morning after the birth, I fed my son and held him in the basin whilst Anushka poured warm salty water over his skin. At first, he screamed, but soon after, he settled to enjoy the warmth of the water and wriggled from side to side. We both laughed and then she started to sing. The night had been long; he fed every hour. I did not complain, I was too full of joy to dwell on the tiredness that came from a sleepless night.

"Why don't you give him to me. You need some sleep my queen."

I smiled at her and shook my head. I knew she was right, I was tired, but I was waiting to hold him next to me so we could sleep together. I could not bear for him to be too far away from me. She shrugged and laughed. I wondered how she knew so much about babies and childbirth as she did not have any children of her own. Before I got a chance to ask, there was three loud knocks on the door.

We both looked at each other, puzzled. Who could be calling? Anushka continued with the bath with some haste, her hands soaked in water and sea salt. The knocking persisted, so I immediately took the baby. "Go, answer, it might be Eliana with news from the king." I could not think of anyone else who would bring such noise at a time when I was to be at rest. It had to be urgent. Panic creeped in as I wondered if all was well with the King. The feasting had carried on late into the evening, the music filling the palace and I had heard the living quarters were filled with gifts from both within the palace and the people of Israel.

When Anushka returned, her face was drained and white. "Your grandfather seeks your urgent attention my queen. He says you must come to him at once." My heart squeezed tight reminding me of the pangs of childbirth still fresh in my memory. Why would my Saba need to see me? What was so urgent that he risked being ceremoniously unclean until the evening? He knew that I had just given birth and would be in *Niddah,* bleeding. Also, I was not strong on my feet yet and still exhausted from my sleepless night. However, I had to respond to his summons.

Anushka swaddled the baby, laid him on the bed, and helped me to dress. I placed a veil over my head and walked slowly. The distance from my inner chambers to the living quarters seemed to have doubled in length. Two of the servant-girls were waiting to support me as I approached my Saba. I bowed my head in greeting, unable to kneel, but my slave girls fell at his feet and he nodded his understanding. I walked slowly towards the red cushion, mindful of the eyes that watched me; I knew something terrible had happened. I just did not know what. With care, I was lowered to a position of rest, sitting as far away from my Saba as I could, but close enough so he did not need to raise his voice.

"Leave us be," he commanded.

I looked at my Saba's face, confused. Taking deep breaths, I sat patiently, not wanting to usher in the bad news.

Silence hung heavy in the air as my Saba stared beyond the walls, not speaking. "Is the boy well?" He finally spoke, his head lowered like one in great sorrow.

"Yes, my lord, he is small but strong and now asleep," I responded. I rested easy, leaning back a bit, satisfied that his visit was born out of concern for the early birth. Perhaps, the King had sent him to bring word to me. "Is the King well my lord?" I asked, wanting to end the continued silence.

Saba raised his hand and placed it on his head and then spat on the ground. "A great sin has occurred in this palace and Yahweh has spoken. That which was hidden has now been revealed. No, the King is not well. He lies on his face crying out to the Lord as we speak."

I sat up too quickly and winced in pain. I could hear my heartbeat as it thudded within my breast. I placed my hand on my chest trying to stop it from breaking free.

"Tell me Bathsheba, this child born to the King, is it early as was spoken?"

I shifted in my seat, my throat now burning; no words could escape from my mouth. What had happened? Where was this questioning coming from? I held on to my words, not wanting to be too quick to speak.

"Speak the truth, Bathsheba, the prophet of the Lord has already visited the house of the king in the early hours of the morning."

I knew I needed to respond to him and quickly. By now, I could already imagine and hear whispers on the other side of the door. News was spreading and spreading fast.

"My son is born of the King and everything that was said is as it has been said."

I am not sure if it was anger, disappointment, or confusion, but the look on my Saba's face was unlike any I had ever seen before. He held his first finger to his cheek in deep contemplation, as though he was trying to solve a puzzle that made no sense. He looked at me and said, "So why then did the king put the sword of the Ammonites to Uriah's neck?"

I held on to the cushion tightly as the room began to spin around me. What was it my grandfather had just said? I shook my head to steady my vision and tapped my ears with force; I was hearing and seeing things. "My lord, have you misspoken?" My voice was barely a whisper.

"The prophet of Yahweh visited the palace this morning requesting urgent presence with the King. The elders of the house had just gathered to discuss matters of people and the report that came from war. When the presence of Nathan was announced, the king welcomed him with much gladness, speaking boldly of the news of the boy. A seat was set before him, but he refused to take it; instead, the prophet turned his face to the king and spoke a parable. He told the king of a rich man with many flocks and herds, and a poor man who had nothing except one small lamb, one which the poor man had cared for like a child from birth. When the rich man was visited by a traveller, he planned a meal to welcome him. Instead of taking from one of his many flocks, he took the small lamb, the only one the poor man had and cooked that as a meal for his guest. The King burned with anger at the injustice as did we the elders. Who would do such a wicked thing? We wondered! The King spoke with an oath that the man who had done this wicked thing shall not only be put to death but repay with four folds that which he had taken." He stopped as though he needed to catch his breath.

I certainly needed to release mine. Could such wickedness still exist amongst God's people? What injustice had just been spoken in my ears? "The king has judged correctly, my lord," I said. But what did all of this have to do with me? Surely, my Saba had not come to discuss matters of the kingdom with me. When he cleared his throat, I knew there was more to the story than had already been shared.

Saba shook his head and pushed his feet aside; it was then I noticed his hands were shaking. "The prophet Nathan pointed to the King and said, you are the man." He said, "You have killed Uriah the Hittite; you have stolen his wife and have killed him by the sword of the people of Ammon." He paused to shake his head, spitting on the floor again. "We the elders, seven in number, stood with our face to the ground at the word of the prophet. Then we raised our heads and our eyes turned to the King. From his own lips we heard, 'I have sinned against the Lord' and the matter was confirmed as truth. Uriah the Hittite was killed at the word of the King"

I stared at him, confused, afraid, and angry at the same time. The death of my husband Uriah was at the hand of the King. He defiled me, then killed my husband and took me as his wife. I screamed with fury from the pit of my stomach as a fresh wave of grief filled me. I was the little lamb, taken from the man who had one by the man who had many. I heard my son cry and my bosom responded, milk poured freely and I yearned to feed my son, the only good thing that had come of this terrible situation.

My Saba turned his head towards the infant's cry, and I hoped he would dismiss me. I had heard enough for the day. I longed to go into my inner chamber and weep for my husband, his life taken away from him by the same man I had now given mine to. Bitterness rose to my lips, and I too spat on the floor.

Instead of being dismissed, my Saba drew near to me and continued to speak. "The Lord has spared the life of the King; he would not be put to death for his sin; but a curse has been placed on his household and the son..." He paused, looking at me, this time, his eyes filled with tears. He moved even closer to where I sat and then he took my hands in his, declaring himself unclean immediately. "Bathsheba, this thing has greatly displeased the Lord. The prophet has spoken from the heart of God. That which was done in secret has now been brought to light."

The tears flowed freely now and I looked around me as I remembered the word of Yahweh, the one who sees; the one who is everywhere. Can anyone hide from his presence? I did not have much time to gather my thoughts or my words before Saba continued to speak.

"The prophet, Nathan, he said..." My Saba stammered although not one to be short of words.

My heart sank; what more needed to be said? My shame would be scattered like litter on the streets of Jerusalem by now. The quiet voices far behind me in the living quarters already spoke loudly enough.

"He said so that the name of Yahweh will not be blasphemed by His enemies, the life of your son has been requested by God, atonement for the sin of the king."

Chapter Thirty-Eight

I awoke many hours later with a head that felt heavier than the rock that sat just outside the cooking quarters in the house of Uriah; the one I had rested on many evenings to feel the cool breeze as Anushka baked bread or roasted lamb. I remembered little of how I got into my own bed; the last memory I had was of a painful dream, one in which my Saba had told me the king had killed my husband and my son was going to die.

"Noooooooooooooooooo," I screamed, trying to raise myself from the bed.

Anushka rushed to my side pushing me back to lay down. "My queen, please, you must rest, please," she said. She hastened to bring my son to me. When she placed him at my bosom, I felt the heat from his skin burn next to mine. Darkness now filled the room, and I called for the lamp so I could see him. I wept when I saw his face red with fever and a rash had spread across his forehead. I unwrapped him from the cloth that held him bound and immediately saw the same purple rash all over his body, his arms were weak and his mouth closed.

"Adonai, You asked me to forgive him, why can't You forgive him too? Why would You do this wicked thing and take my son from me? Take me instead, take my life and let him have his, I beg You, please take me." I lifted my son, rose from the bed, and fell to my knees, crying and begging God for his life.

Beside me, I heard Anushka scream; she fell to her knees also and prayed. "Take me too, Yahweh, only spare this child. I am a mere slave, not worthy of the life of the king's son, but if you add my life to that of my queen, perhaps we can pay the price for his. Please Yahweh, now I call You my God, take my life and spare this child"

We remained on our knees the whole night crying out to God. I stopped only to try to feed my son; his mouth opened a little and he suckled softly, sleeping more than he was eating. He was too weak to cry. I was too afraid to be angry with Yahweh. I needed His mercy much more than I needed to feel wrath. I could not even grieve for Uriah and all my Saba had said concerning his death. I shifted to one side, my heart focused on pleading for mercy for my son. Why did he have to suffer for the sin of the king? He was the only joy I had in my life, perfect from birth, innocent of everything. My mind wandered back to my second month, when, as a woman with child, I took an offering to the priest at his tent as one unclean to hide the sin. It was the day Salma came to visit.

I started to plead for the Lord's forgiveness for my own sin; my hands were not clean either. I had covered the truth to save my own life; it was not just about my son, if I was to speak the truth, it was for my own sake too. I wanted to live to be a mother to my child and if Uriah had come home, I would have given him this child as his, even though in my heart I had said I would not. "Yahweh, You are the one who sees the heart of man; You are the one who is everywhere and knows every-thing, search me and see my own fault and place it on my head, please, do not take the life of my son." I prayed this fervent prayer not once but many times for the next three days. I kept praying but Yahweh did not speak.

On the fourth day since my Saba brought the word of the Lord, I sat on the floor, my son on a blanket between my legs. By now, he had stopped nursing, only his shallow breathing told me there was still life in him. He slept and only cried out gently when touched. The purple rash did not become sores, I was thankful for that. Though he was weak, he was not in pain, he did not seem uneasy. He seemed at peace. Yahweh did not cause him to suffer. For this, I was grateful. I could not eat; I could not sleep either. I just cried bitter tears.

I heard from Eliana that the king had not eaten in four days. Since the prophet visited, he had lain on the bare ground crying out to the Lord for his son's life. He refused to eat or drink even at the word of his elders. They feared for his life. I did not. At that moment, I prayed that he would die. Let him carry his own sin, let his wickedness fall on his own head. My desire was for my son and my son only. I could not see past the pain in my heart.

All these months, planning, plotting, praying, all for what? This could not be the end. I shook my sleeping son, urging him to respond. My breasts were very heavy with milk, and I grieved with tears each time I had to press milk into a cup instead of my son's mouth. The news of the king's sin had not spread as much as I imagined: only the elders knew and a few slaves. My grandfather had sent word that a careless word spoken would result in death. The matter had been judged rightly by God and should be rested. Nothing more was said. The word that was now spoken was that the King's infant son, born two months early had taken with fever and all should pray for mercy from Yahweh.

On the fifth day since my Saba brought the news, I arose with a heavy heart. The night before had been filled with dreams of Uriah's blood crying out to God for mercy. I was at war with him in my dream, pulling my son away from the earth that spoke his name. I continued to plead with Yahweh, calling his name while awake as I did whilst asleep. I had still not heard the voice of the lord. Certainly not in the way I had all this while; there was not even a firefly in sight. I felt abandoned by my God. I needed him. I wanted answers I wanted his forgiveness. I wanted his mercy.

My son, who now rested beside me, cried out and I immediately picked him up and held him close. He turned his head from left to right, his mouth opening in a suckling motion. I lifted him to my bosom, and he began to suckle. I praised Yahweh. Perhaps my prayers were not answered but the king was on his face, still crying out to God and He had heard him. I knew the favour of the Lord rested on the king. It was why he had not been struck dead for his sin.

I called for Anushka to bring me dry bread and raisin tea. As my son nursed, I chewed the bread to give me strength. I had eaten very little in five days and was weak from crying and praying. The baby nursed for over an hour and shortly after his bowels exploded giving a foul odour. They had been closed for days, as he ate nothing; only a few sips of spring water passed his lips. I sang praises to Yahweh as I took great joy in cleansing my son. Even the purple rash had dulled to a dark-red colour and much of his skin looked clearer.

Eliana visited again, this time, her hands were full of fresh food from the king's quarters. "He still refuses to eat. Night and day, he lies on the bare ground, crying out to Yahweh on behalf of this child. Never have I seen such love of a father," she said, laying the basket of food at my feet.

The smell of freshly roasted lamb with honey called to my stomach which grumbled in protest at the lack of nutrients. I ate freely, needing strength to feed the infant that was now asleep at my bosom. Moments earlier, he had been soaked in fresh goats' milk, to soothe the rash on his skin. I paid little attention to the conversation between Eliana and Anushka as my thoughts were rioting. Bitterness and sorrow tasted like dust in my mouth. A gentle breeze filled the room which surprised me as the windows were shut. With the breeze came a whisper:

"The one who takes is the one who gives, be at peace my child."

I shook my head, trying to reassure myself that I had not heard the voice of the Lord. I thought that prayers had been answered, maybe not mine, but at least the prayers of Yahweh's chosen servant, the king. So why was the Lord revealing Himself as the one who takes? "Take what, my God?" I whispered. Surely not my son!

I looked down at him; he was fast asleep, his breathing easy. He was beautiful to behold, his face exactly like his father's. The king had not seen him because we planned on hiding the truth. If he was a healthy baby born at the right time, he would have been taken straight to his father after he had been cleansed with salt and had taken his first milk. But because he was spoken as one born before his time and was weak, the plan was to place him in the King's arms on the eighth day of his birth for circumcision. This was a ritual that must be followed according to the law of Moses without fail.

How far would this deception have carried and at great cost? We had put all these plans in place, yet Yahweh watched in silence with His own plans. "Yahweh, please keep him alive to feel the hands of his father." I prayed over him. I wanted the king to see him, to touch him, to bless him. "Yahweh, You said I should forgive the king, please forgive him." I prayed and His response was quick ,*"I have shown mercy on my servant, the king. He lives."*

Chapter Thirty-Nine

T he sixth day after I heard the news from my Saba was much like the fifth. My son looked stronger, and spent most of the day eating, much to my surprise and to the surprise of the people around me. Eliana visited again, with word that the king had still not risen from the floor and no food or drink had passed his lips. His elders were worried and two of his servants had taken to the floor beside him, begging him to rise and eat. But the king's response was tears and prayers. He spoke to no one but God.

Though my heart was bitter and angry, it was drawn towards the king. The way he prayed for his son, refusing to accept the word of the prophet brought some comfort to my soul. I remembered with fondness the way he spoke to his son, kissing my stomach tenderly and laughing each time the baby kicked at his open palm placed gently on my stomach. He had shown so much love to this boy even before he was born and now, he prayed fervently for his life. My heart was softened towards him; I longed to speak words of comfort, to tell him that our son was nursing again and the rash was easing. I longed to tell him Yahweh had heard his cry and to wipe the tears from his face.

I did not know that anger and love could exist in the same place until I found myself grieving for the dead and longing for the living at the same time. I remembered the rosebush, a reminder that beauty and pain could exist in the same space. Mixed emotions rushed through me. I moved from anger to sorrow, to guilt, to shame: all in the space of mere moments, not settling on how I truly felt. Yahweh knew the truth from the beginning, even before he asked me to forgive the King. How could I now hold on to bitterness? But what about Uriah? What about the life of my son who was destined to pay the price of a sin he was innocent of?

When my infant son screamed, my heart leapt with joy. His voice carried weight and he cried until he was changed from the soiled cloth that brought him much discomfort. After that, he suckled for a long time until sleep came, and he rested in my arms again.

"It appears his strength has returned; Yahweh has been gracious." Anushka whispered the words my heart had been too afraid to speak.

"Should I send word to the king?" asked, Eliana, excitement adding shrillness to her voice.

"No, not yet," I insisted. My spirit resisted sharing the news of my son's progress. I looked at him; unnamed, deciding what I would call him. I had waited, wanting his father to send word of his name. It was not uncommon for children to be named by their mothers as well as their fathers. A child often had more than one name. "What should I call him?" I turned to the slave women who had become like sisters.

"He looks exactly like his father." Eliana chuckled and Anushka nodded in agreement.

"Well then, I will name him after his father, David." I whispered the name into his ears and kissed his cheek. The boy startled and screamed with soft tears, annoyed to be disturbed from his sleep. We laughed at the disdainful look on his face; such emotions from one so young. Then I laid him down to sleep.

The seventh day since my Saba brought news came, and I woke up with hope in my heart. At last, the King would be forced to rise from the floor to circumcise his son. It was the eighth day since his birth. As the sun rose, so did my household, everyone getting ready for the occasion. By this time, I was no longer unclean. However, I would still not be able to enter the House of the Lord to witness the circumcision of my son. For that, I was grateful as I could not bear to see him in pain. According to the custom, I was to wait thirty-three more days to be purified from my bleeding. I could not touch anything sacred, including the king, or enter the Lord's Sanctuary.

On the fortieth day after the birth of my son, I would take a year-old lamb for a burnt offering and a pigeon for a sin offering to the priest at the entrance of the tent. Only then would I be purified and cleansed. I decided in my heart that I would take two lambs and two pigeons. There was much I needed to be cleansed of. My heart was bitter.

I picked up my son to nurse him as his night had been restless. He cried more than he ate. I welcomed his warm body to my bosom, and he suckled without delay. There was a basin of fresh warm water with dried herbs waiting to cleanse him. A new blanket had been laid out for him, woven with soft wool from the skin of a young lamb. As he nursed, he relieved himself loudly and I smiled at my son. "David," I whispered.

By the time I placed him in Anushka's hands he was well fed, and he settled into the bath, sucking his fingers as the warm water washed over his skin. His skin was then covered in scented oil making it soft to touch, and slippery as well. When she placed him back in my arms, I held him tightly, drinking in the smell of him; he smelled of wildflowers. I brushed his long hair away from his face and filled it with kisses. David was fast asleep, even before he was covered in his new blanket.

Dawn was now present, the sun fully awake in the sky. I rocked the already sleeping baby in my arms, trying my best not to sing. When I sang to him a few nights previously, the poor child cried. I scared myself almost as much as I scared him.

I loved the weight of his small body in my arms, this was the moment I had dreamed of and prayed for. I loved the smell of him, the way his tiny fist curled around my first finger, the way his mouth opened and closed every time he searched for food, everything about him I loved.

As I sat down and placed him on my lap, my face turned towards heaven and I called on Yahweh with thanksgiving. As though in response to my praise, I heard a faint cry and my son started to shiver in my arms. I stood up and started rocking him again, calling out to Anushka who had gone to empty the basin of water. His breathing continued to be fast and heavy, his little chest rising and falling quickly. I must have started screaming as, in mere moments, my inner chamber was filled with the girls who waited outside my door.

I do not know the exact moment life left his body, but I remember seeing his head fall to the side and suddenly I was standing outside the door, watching myself hold my dead son in my arms, screaming.

Chapter Forty

The days that followed his death were dark, cold, and lonely. Words failed me. My tiny frame was quickly becoming a shadow, my legs too weak to carry me. Anything I managed to eat or drink was quickly expelled by my body that refused any food. I grieved for my son and for my life that seemed useless to both man and God. I begged Yahweh to take me home, but His silence was a painful blow; even He did not want me. Once, I placed all the herbs used for the pain of child-birth into a cup and drank it all at once hoping it would kill me.

Disappointment washed over me the next morning as my eyes opened and my stomach roiled for days with much pain. Death would have been kinder but it did not come to me.

By now, I had resigned myself to a life of constant sorrow. It felt like each time something good happened, something bad followed. First, I was raped, and then given a gift of a child, the one thing my heart had craved. I welcomed the news with both sorrow and joy. Then I was bereaved, my husband of many years, the one who made my heart sing was gone, killed at war, leaving me a widow, pregnant and alone with death waiting for me. But then I was redeemed and brought into the palace, a crown placed on my head, and I became a queen. Then I was rejected by the King, not called into his presence for over six months, laughed at by my own slaves. But God smiled on me with courage and my simple gift brought me into the arms of the man I despised, and, in his arms, I found love like I had never known before, and joy came at last. My head was covered, my son and I would live. Then, I became a mother, birthing a handsome son, and my joy knew no limits. I rejoiced in my heart that day and night but soon after, sadness came with the revelation that I was married to a murderer, the one who had taken my husband's life and mine. My son, born of sin, was taken by Yahweh. I had nothing left to live for, tormented by the words of Yahweh that played constantly in my mind:

"The one who takes is the one who gives, be at peace my child," he had said. But I was not at peace, far from it. His words made no sense to me; the one who takes is the one who gives? I pondered them in my heart over and over again. All I could see with my red eyes and ash covered face was a God who takes and he had taken my source of hope leaving my heart broken into irreparable pieces.

———

I had heard no word from the King, not because he did not send it, but because I was unwilling to listen. Each time I saw Eliana, I turned my back to her immediately, so she knew I was unwilling to hear any word that came from the king. I did not care if that was the message she sent back to the king. I knew he would not come himself. He could not. I was not purified yet.

As the weeks passed, my anger shifted to grief and again the Lord whispered, *"Forgive him."* Yet, I clutched my bitterness tight against my chest like my son's blanket, the one that had been laid out for him to be covered in for the circumcision that never happened. I was not going to forgive and I made my intentions quite clear. There was just too much now to forgive.

I sat by the window and looked out into the palace courtyard. My thoughts were empty, my eyes leaked without prompting. The tears never dried. I watched as people moved. I saw women with baskets on their heads in the far distance heading towards the market. I saw children running down the streets. A young boy with a cage full of birds stood at the palace gates talking to Three foot soldiers. All before me were people doing life, living life as though nothing had happened. Their life continued whilst mine stopped. It did not seem fair.

"Sin will not go unpunished, my child. Each man must endure the consequences for the choices he makes. But my grace will abound." Yahweh's word came without invitation; the explanation of my plight brought me little comfort. I understood the meaning of His words: the sin of the king should not go unpunished, but in punishing the king, He punished me as well. It was not only the king who suffered the consequences of his choice: Uriah suffered; I suffered; and the king's household, I was told, was going to suffer too. How could one man's choice carry so much pain? If only we could weigh the decisions we make and the sorrow we could cause not only in our own lives, but in the lives of the people we love.

When I finally found the words to enquire about the king, I wished I had not. I wept aloud when I was told the response to the news of our son's death. Anushka recounted the story in detail as she had heard it from Eliana who had heard it from her older brother Michael who was one of the king's foot soldiers. He was one of the three that stood guard outside the door of the king's inner chamber and also at the door of the throne room.

"My queen, there was no one willing to tell the king his son was dead for they were all afraid of what he might do or whose life would be cut short for bearing such news. Who would dare to tell the king his son was dead? A boy he had fasted and prayed for, for the last seven days? When the King had seen many gather with silent whispers, he asked, 'Is the boy dead?' To which they replied 'Yes, he is dead.' Once the news was confirmed, the king picked himself from the ground and walked straight into his living quarters in the west wing of the palace. There, he washed himself, anointed his head with oil, put on a fresh new robe and went into the House of the Lord and worshipped for hours. When he returned from the Tabernacle, he called for a huge feast to be laid before him and he ate to his fill".

I gasped in pain and astonishment. "Does he not have remorse for the death of his son that he washes his head and eats to his fill?" I felt betrayed. In my eyes, it felt as though the memory of my son was easily tossed away.

"I hear even the elders were also filled with surprise, my queen. The words came from your grandfather who inquired of the king saying, 'While the boy lived, you neither ate nor drank for seven days, your face was flat, and your body was on the hard ground weeping before the Lord. And now, your son is dead, and you no longer mourn, instead you eat?' To this, the king replied, 'While my son lived, I wept before the Lord with fasting and prayers. I thought, maybe His grace would find me and His mercy would let the child live. But now, he is dead, why should I mourn and fast? No tears can bring him back. I will go to him one day, but he cannot come back to me."

The truth in his words stung me to my core. There was wisdom in them but I was unwilling to see it or hear it. I wanted his heart to remain broken for the child, as mine was. But could his grief be as much as mine? He had many other sons, I had just this one and he was gone. No, I would not forgive him.

Chapter Forty-One

Forty-one days had passed since the birth of my son. I could not believe it when Anushka told me. The day before, Eliana had come to visit; this time, I managed a smile when all she brought was a huge basket of fresh grapes but made no attempt to speak. I did see her and Anushka in quiet conversation for many minutes, but I had too much to consider in my own mind to wonder what it was they discussed. I enjoyed the sweet grapes as I needed the strength brought by food. The things for my purification had already been prepared. At my request, two one-year old lambs were placed in the king's chariot as well as two doves and two pigeons.

I looked outside my window, longing to feel grass beneath my feet. It amazed me the things that I missed besides the grass beneath my feet. I missed the various sounds that filled the market square, even the smell of cattle. I had not left the palace gates for many months, and I looked forward to the short trip to the tent of the priest. However, in truth, I wanted to go back home, back to the house of Uriah.

Life in the palace held no appeal for me. I craved for something from long ago, a time in my life when I knew peace. I hungered for peace. I was tired, my heart was weak, my body was weaker, and my life seemed to be leaving me behind. I was no queen; I did not want to be one. The crown was the first thing I removed from my head when my son died. I felt as though I no longer needed to wear it. Of what use would I be to the king? I had no son - the one thing that qualified me to be queen - to show. I placed the crown in a linen cloth and then in the huge cedar wood drawer by my bedside.

I felt my empty chest, the place where the necklace the King gifted me, the one with two turtle doves as a pendant with precious stones for eyes. I had worn it every day since the day he gave it to me, not taking it off until our son died. I wrapped it around his neck before his lifeless body was taken away along with my very existence. I was drowning in my own sorrow and I knew if I carried on, grief would kill me quicker than any herbs could.

My head lay in Anushka's arms as I let her wash my hair for the first time since my son's life was taken. Before I stepped into the basin, I had seen my reflection in the mirror, I paused to stare as I did not recognise myself. My beauty was hidden behind red eyes and pale skin barely covered my bones. My body was weak, drained of life. My breasts no longer held any milk. I was glad that my veil would cover my face when I left the palace. No one could see me like this and not weep.

As she washed my hair, my eyes remained closed and I found pleasure in her tender touch on my scalp. I settled into the cool water that filled the basin. Suddenly, Anushka stopped singing much to my displeasure. I sensed she had unspoken words on her lips. "Speak quickly so your song can caress my ears once more." My voice had little weight; my throat, raw from many days of screaming, was still to recover. I spoke only in whispers.

"Every day, Eliana has brought word from the king. He asks how you fare. He has heard the news of your countenance and is troubled by your silence. What word can I send to the king?"

I left her question hanging in the air. I had no response for him. If I sent any word, it would be unkind to his ears. I chose silence instead. "Sing, Anushka." And with that I dismissed the conversation.

Chapter Forty-Two

The gown laid out for me fell loose around my shoulders, so another had to be chosen. Even that one, once tight around my bosom had ample room. I did not realise how frail I had become until I tried on all my outdoor garments, and none would fit. I picked the best of them and carried the loose fabric which flowed around me. The journey to the house of the priest and return tired me. The ritual complete, I was purified in body as the law required. Ashamed of my frail body, I refused to go into the marketplace or step into the field as my feet had longed for. As soon as I returned to the palace, I made my way with much difficulty to my living quarters and immediately took refuge in my inner chambers, closing the door firmly behind me. I climbed in my big bed, placed my face in my pillow, and wept.

When I heard my chamber door open and slam shut, I did not move. I had no energy to exchange more irritable words with Anushka. She had wanted us to take a longer ride around Jerusalem, even up to the mountains. She had suggested I visit my aunty who had been concerned for me for weeks. I shook my head with my disapproval, dismissing every good idea she brought my way. However, the footsteps that walked the distance from the door to my bed hit the ground heavier than Anushka's feet. Before I had the strength to turn, I felt my bed shift under a heavy weight. I smelled him before his hand touched my hair. I felt as if my heart ceased. The king was in my inner chamber and all I wanted to do was run.

His touch was tender, coaxing a response from me, his hand moved from my hair to my face, and I felt him touch my wet cheeks. When his hand met with bone, he moved it quickly over my body as though in search of something to hold. I heard his sandals fall from his feet as he climbed into the bed. He lifted my head carefully, turning my face towards him. His hand removed my hair from my face. I heard him gasp and then his head fell on my chest and he wept loudly, squeezing me hard enough to take what little life I had left in me. I shifted with the little strength I had left, needing room to breathe.

He raised his eyes to mine, then slowly peeled back the covers looking at me from my head all the way down to my toes. I wore only a light tunic. I closed my eyes as the image of my body haunted me. I knew what he saw was mere skin on bones; the beauty he once craved had faded. He spoke words beneath his breath, but I could not hear them. I knew they were not for me; it seemed like he was having a conversation with himself. When he pulled me into his embrace, he was gentle, placing my head on his chest. I was angry. I was in pain. I wanted to fight, to resist him, but I had no strength in me. Although my heart was heavy, his touch made it seem light and I felt something else, peace. My body rested into his and for the first time in forty days, I slept deeply.

When my eyes opened, darkness filled the room; a small lamp gave light in the distance. Everywhere was quiet. I was not alone; the king was still next to me, though this time he laid by my right side.

As soon as I moved, he awoke. "My queen." His voice was tender in my ears. Without waiting for a response, he rose to his feet and walked towards the door. He knocked once and it was opened, a few words were spoken and then he returned to me. Shortly after, the door opened once more, and Eliana walked in with a tray of food and set it on the small table by my bedside. She kindled the coal fire in the wall and the room was flooded with light. She walked towards me, wanting to help me sit but the king turned to her and said, "Leave us." She hastened from the room and closed the door.

My king reached for me, gently pulling me to rise and sit on the red cushion I loved so much. Then, he lifted the small bowl from the golden tray. I looked with horror; I had no desire to eat anything. As though he read my mind, he lowered himself next to me and opened the bowl so I could see the simple bone broth. He fed me slowly, tenderly, patiently. Even when I turned my face after only a few spoons passed my lips, he coaxed me gently to eat some more; and I did. He then poured a goblet full of strong wine and gave it to me to drink.

For the next seven days the king returned to my chamber each evening, just before sunset and he took time to feed me himself and then lay beside me. No words were spoken. When I cried, he cried. For the first time, I considered the grief of the king: he had lost a son too, one he never set eyes on or touched whilst he was alive. The grief was not mine alone. When I slept, he slept. Sometimes, he sang, most times he prayed but each time, he was by my side. His presence brought immeasurable comfort.

As more days passed, my body grew stronger and my cold heart grew warmer. Hope floated again and the word of the Lord came to me once more.

"The one who takes is the one who gives, be at peace."

This time, I held onto the words, pondering them with renewed hope.

If the king who had been openly rebuked in front of his elders with his sin once hidden laid bare before his own advisers … if the king whose son paid the price for his sin … if the king who had also brought a curse on his household and held the weight of the consequences firmly on his shoulders … if this king could still open his mouth and praise Yahweh, then who was I not to?

I had heard the praise on his lips; I had heard the prayers night after night.

I closed my eyes and prayed.

Chapter Forty-Three

The next day, when the king returned to my chambers just before sundown, I was dressed and waiting for him. As the doors opened and he walked in, I rose to my feet to greet him, my voice barely above a whisper as I said, "My king." Even though my throat had now healed, thanks to the balm of honey and lemon that Anushka forced down my throat, my voice was still hoarse and tender.

I was much stronger now, eating more during the day and drinking fresh cool water to revive my muscles and bones and add colour to my skin. I was still a long way from my usual self, but there was more flesh around my bones and the dark circles around my eyes were gone. By now, my head did not hurt so much and my eyes were dry most days. I had taken extra care with my appearance and allowed Anushka to put some colour on my cheeks and lips. I saw delight in his eyes as he saw me and a smile creased the corner of his lips.

He took my hands in his, holding my gaze and then his eyes began to water. I stood, shocked, not sure what to do or say. I had heard him cry on my chest and even as I sat beside him, but now, I was looking at him as the tears trickled down his red cheeks. I raised my hand to his face, pushing the tears away. They confused me. When he opened his mouth to speak, he turned his eyes towards heaven as a prayer left his lips, this time; I listened quietly to the words he spoke before me to Yahweh.

"Let Your mercy fall on me, my God
For You are full of loving kindness,
You have tender mercies in abundance
Wipe away my transgressions.
Wash me deeply from my iniquity,
Clean away my unrighteousness,
To You I confess my wrongdoing,
And now my sin is always before me."

I did not hear the rest of his prayers but many more words were spoken. My heart was moved to deep compassion, his last words a blow to my wounded soul. I was his sin always before him, each day he saw me, he would remember.

"Please Yahweh," I cried out to God. "Help us find a way towards Your peace." I wanted my king to look at me and see more than just sin and I too wanted to look at him without the pain of the past like a dark blanket over my eyes.

When he had silenced from his prayers, he took my hand and led me to the large blue cushion on the other side of my inner chambers, far away from the window and even further from the door. It was a cushion I had sat on only once, preferring the comfort of the familiar red one. This part of my inner chamber felt cold and isolated, although tastefully furnished like the rest of the room. There was a large table not too far away on which our evening meal had been set to rest.

"What happened to your necklace?" He asked, his hand touching the place where it should have been.

"I wrapped it around our son."

He leaned in close. "We are alone, why do you whisper?"

I smiled. "My voice is broken, my lord."

He moved much closer so he could hear me speak without straining his ears.

"He was beautiful, his eyes dark brown just like yours."

I felt his hand run up and down my arm. "The prophet, Nathan, he brought many words from God. The consequence of my sin, my head and heart will carry throughout my lifetime."

With each word he spoke my heart grieved, but nothing grieved me more than when he spoke of the boy.

"I saw your face, Bathsheba." His hands reached out and he drew a circle around my face.

I remembered the feel of his body against my open palm and my heart was crushed within me.

"I've sinned against the Lord; I took away your husband and then your child."

I wanted to ask him why, but I knew I had no right to question the king. Besides, the reason changed nothing. I rested my head on his right shoulder. I did not know what to say.

"When I heard of your distress," he said, "I prayed every day for you that the Lord would keep you in good health. When you sent no response to my greetings, at first, I was angry. It was the people that felt the weight of it as I judged harshly and spoke loudly. But then, my dreams were filled with your tears and my heart burned for you. I counted the forty days till I could hold you, on my hands and toes; every day was too long to bear. And then the day came, and I rushed quickly to you but when I set my eyes upon you...." His voice broke and his tears wet my hair. "It was like I saw the face of death, my queen. You were fading away before my eyes and it was my doing. All this pain you feel, I have laid at your feet."

I lifted my head from his shoulder and placed my finger on his lips. "No more, my king. Let us leave the past for the Lord who has judged rightly." I wrapped my arms around him as tightly as I could, and we sat lost in our own thoughts.

My stomach grumbled, breaking the silence, we untangled and started to eat the food that had now gone cold. Three knocks on the door and Eliana entered the room with a tray filled with a fresh jug of water, raisin tea and cakes. After she set it down, she bowed to the king and asked. "Should I call for the harpist, my king?"

He nodded. Shortly after, sweet music filled my room from the other side of the inner chamber door and we ate without words.

Chapter Forty-Four

I awoke to the king's touch as he lifted me from the cushion to my bed. I had fallen asleep as the music brought comfort to my soul. I smiled and turned to him after he laid me down.

"You are awake," he whispered, stroking my hair gently. I saw the passion in his eyes, his hunger for me was not hidden. Suddenly, he tilted his head to look at me, as though he wanted to see me from a different angle, or something had occurred to him. He looked around the room, his eyes searching. They alighted on a table with a huge mirror hung above it. The table was filled with various creams, oils, brushes, and paints.

There were hooks on both sides of the mirror where different coloured veils flowed, and an opulent wooden box was filled with jewellery. He stood up and walked to the table to examine what was on it, his eyes still searching. He returned to my side. "Where is your crown?"

My hand went straight to my head as though I expected it to be there, and then I remembered. "I removed it from my head when David died."

The king winced at the sound of his name on my lips and withdrew from me. His eyes flashed red. I pulled my hands to my mouth and covered it and shook my head when the realisation dawned on me.

"No, my king. I beg your forgiveness, not you, my lord. A few days before he died, your son seemed like he had gained strength; he was nursing again, the fever had cooled and the purple rash that plagued his skin had changed colour. I thought he would live and realised I had not named him. At the time I was with both Eliana and Anushka. I asked them, what name befits the boy and they both agreed he looked just like you and it was so that I named him after you."

His expression changed at my words and the peace returned. "Why did you remove your crown?"

I did not want to lie and I feared to speak the truth but I spoke it anyway. "I thought I would no longer have need of it. The son that earned me a place at the palace was no more so I thought I would be cast aside."

The King stared at me, his left hand underneath his chin, as though he pondered my words. "Bring your crown, Bathsheba," he commanded.

I jumped up and hurried to the place I kept it but it was not there. I searched frantically, turning the cloth upside down and inside out. I opened every single drawer of the huge cedar cabinet by my bedside, but it was not there. The cloth I had tied it in I tossed to the floor.

I stood with my hands empty, in the middle of the room staring at the king. He did not move; he just waited and watched me. Panic gripped me. By now, the house was asleep; Anushka would surely know where my crown was. I waited, hoping the king would dismiss the need for it till the morning, but he said nothing; he just stared across the room towards the dressing table he had walked away from only moments ago. His hand still held his chin.

"Yahweh, please help me," I whispered in silent prayer.

I turned to look at the mirror and something glistened, catching my eye. I walked toward it and right on top of my purple veil lay my crown, the precious stones twinkling a reflection on the mirror.

Joy filled my heart as I picked it up, touching the doves on either side. I was so thankful to see it. I turned to show it to the king. A mischievous smile twitched on his lips. My mouth opened in shock. All this while he watched me search frantically, sweating with fear and he knew exactly where it was; he had seen it. I walked towards him with a light heart. "Have you no mercy, my King?" and he opened his hands to me, and I placed the crown in his palms.

He arose to stand beside me, and I raised my eyes to meet his gaze.

"Bathsheba." He uttered my name gently. "You are not a queen because my son filled your womb, you are *my* queen." He paused to place his hand on his chest, not once, but three times. Looking into my very soul he continued. "I chose you and I married you because I love you. I placed the crown upon your head and that means you are my queen, now and always." Then, he replaced the crown firmly on my head.

How could I have been so foolish? Allowing my fear to speak to me, to deceive me. The king loved me and I loved him too. When he bent towards me, I leaned forward on my toes, meeting his lips with such force I swayed. He caught and held me. Love tasted so sweet. I stood as he undressed me, removing everything except my crown, he picked me up and laid me gently on the bed, reminding me with every touch how much I was the queen he loved. That night, he vowed with an oath that after me, he would take no other and he spoke words of love to me. And when I called him "My king," he shook his head and said, "No. My love," he whispered. "Call me my love." Then he placed my hands in his hair, I ran my fingers through his thick mane, and he moaned softly. Then, he kept me awake until the break of dawn.

Love was indeed a balm that soothed the soul, and I came to learn that when love was used as medicine, it had the power to give life in a way that anger and unforgiveness never could. I missed my son and I missed Uriah, but I had come to accept the life that Yahweh had given me. I stopped trying to judge which life was better. I stopped myself from longing for things I could not change, and I adjusted to and embraced life at the palace. I was the king's eighth wife and though it was painful, I had to learn to share his time.

More than a week went by before I saw the king again and when we were alone, I told him how much I missed him.

He looked at me and said, "My queen, you will always have my audience. Do you not know how long you have had my heart? If you need me, call me. Only God and war will keep me away from you."

I smiled knowing I was truly his love.

A few weeks later, Anushka pointed out that my monthly period was a stranger. I held on to my stomach with my eyes wide open. Could it be? That same gentle breeze from many months ago filled the room, bringing back the memory of Yahweh's word to me:

"The one who takes is the one who gives..."

"Oh, Yahweh!" I cried, falling to my knees, praying and praising God. I waited another four weeks before I finally told the King. I wanted two full months to come and go so I was certain of the truth of the child that grew within me.

I sent word, inviting the king for a banquet in my quarters. When the servant returned to say the king would attend, I spent the day with my servants making his favourite meal of wild game, unleavened bread, fish stew and raisin cakes. He loved my raisin cakes.

The evening soon came, and I was dressed and ready to serve my King. I waited till the meal was served and he had been well fed and watered. He knew I enjoyed hearing him speak, so he told me more stories and I sat and listened enraptured. Though my health had returned, my voice did not recover, and I could still barely speak above a whisper. It was a pleasure for me to listen and not speak. He spoke of the war in Ammon that still continued and then of previous wars. I asked him again to tell me the story of killing the Philistine giant, Goliath, and laughed so hard my stomach hurt. After the meal was cleared, we were finally alone, the door of my inner chamber shut firmly.

"So, my queen, to what do I owe the pleasure of your company tonight? Speak freely, what is your heart's desire? My heart is pleased with you, now ask me anything, even half of my kingdom and I will give it to you this night." He spoke the words into my ears and kissed them gently.

"I have no request from my love; instead, I have a gift of good news to bring." I smiled and waited for him to speak.

"What is this news that brings out the colour in your eyes and cheeks and adds sparkle to those same eyes. Tell me quickly."

I enjoyed his eagerness and thought to make him wait a bit longer. "Think of it, my king, suggest something to me."

He paused, and I gave him room to ponder.

"Has your health fully recovered? You look well, with more meat on your bones than before..." He chose silence over the rest of his words, our eyes met with understanding, and we shared a moment of remembrance.

He searched my face for answers; I could see the curiosity that filled his eyes. He brought his lips to mine, kissing me tenderly. "Is this the good news, that your bones burn with passion for me, meaning you could not wait for me to summon you myself?" He teased. "I told you the truth my queen, you will always have my audience," he said, pulling me closer.

I laughed and pushed him away. "You are no good at suggesting, my love. Though there is truth in the two things you have said, that is not the reason why my heart cries out to Yahweh with much praise." I took both his hands in mine and brought them and placed them carefully on my abdomen.

His eyes immediately widened and then filled with tears as the news dawned on him. He rubbed his hand gently across my abdomen before he kissed it firmly and pulled me towards himself. He whispered, "The one who takes is also the one who gives, praise be to God." A cold shiver ran down my spine as I heard him speak the exact words Yahweh had spoken to me. The same God who spoke to me, spoke to him. Indeed, the God I served was everywhere.

Chapter Forty-Five

The months came and went quickly, and the baby grew. I had no strong conviction as to whether I carried a boy or a girl, but I prayed for a son. To birth a son would be God's mercy towards me. This child was already a blessing, but another son would wipe my tears away. The ease with which the child rested surprised me. Unlike the other warrior I carried, this baby was calm, moving little and sleeping a lot although he responded to his father's touch and would wake up to the sound of his voice. When the king kissed my stomach, the baby would turn and turn ever so gently. I convinced myself that I carried a girl.

In the eighth month of my pregnancy, I lay in the king's quarters; for three weeks I had not left his side.

"Has the Lord not told you if the baby you carry is a son or a daughter? Last time you were so sure it was a son, and you were right."

I shook my head with despair. "This time, the Lord is silent, and I am not certain. The baby is quiet; he is not at war within

216 · AMANDA BEDZRAH

me, but will awaken to your voice and touch. If I was to suggest, I would say it is a girl and she will steal her father's heart away from me."

His laughter bounced off the ceiling and echoed through the large room. "My heart is big enough to love you both." His response irritated me without reason. I scolded myself, surely, I should not have envy towards my own daughter. Still, I prayed for a son.

"Bathsheba." I turned to face the king in shock. He had not spoken my name in months. Fear flitted across my face.

"If you carry a daughter, she will be welcomed as a royal princess, a special gift from God. God has blessed me with many sons, I am certain my daughter Tamar would indulge the presence of another girl. But if you carry a son, my queen, I swear to you this, on the life of this child you carry, before the very ears of Yahweh, I will make him the heir to the throne after me. He will be the next king of Israel." He placed his right hand on my stomach and the child leapt at his touch.

I stared at the king, tears filling my eyes and overflowing as the weight of his word to me took root in my brain. I took the words knowing that he spoke the truth of his heart; I did not need to press further. His oath was enough. The King had spoken.

In my ninth month, I returned to my new living quarters in the place he had originally intended for me. Every inch of that room mirrored the king's personal chamber. It was as though I had fallen asleep in one bed and woken up in the exact same bed but in a different room.

Being so close to the king had many advantages. I saw him most days. I shared meals with him even on the days I did not share a bed with him. He visited often, sometimes in the morning and again in the evening. While I revelled in his attention, there were also disadvantages to being so close: I was more aware of when he was not alone and in the company of another of the queens and often wondered if he used the same tender words to them as he spoke to me. I had not yet learnt to curb my jealousy, and I doubted I ever would, but I had learnt to live with it and embrace my predicament.

On one of our many nights of long conversations, I questioned how God made the hearts of men so different from that of women. I told him that a woman would love one man and be satisfied, unlike a man who could love more than one woman. The king did not agree with my reasoning. He insisted that love was different from duty and a man should fulfil the responsibilities of a husband irrespective of love. If this were not the case, widows redeemed by relatives would not be able to bear sons. But then he said, "My queen, what we have goes beyond the call of duty. My heart is in your hands, my soul has been bound to yours from the first day I saw you. Set your mind at rest, my Bathsheba. Only one woman has ever laid hands on my head, and she lives to continue to be loved by me."

Chapter Forty-Six

As the sun sank below the horizon, the pangs of childbirth gripped me. The king had just arrived at my living quarters where a meal had been set. He had not even had time to remove his sandals to wash his feet before I bent over as pain gripped me and I let out a deep sigh. He rushed towards me and held my hand and I squeezed his tightly waiting for the wave of pain to come and go. I settled into gasping breaths. My water had not broken, so I thought it was just an unexpected pain and the baby was still not ready. The ninth month had not been complete, there were still ten days left in the month.

As I lowered myself to sit at the table, I felt another sharp pain. This time, I screamed, grabbing on to the edge of the table and moving my body from side to side. From the corner of my eye, I could see the king's face, white with shock or concern, I was not sure. Anushka threw open the door and rushed to my side, her eyes careful not to meet the king's. She bowed to him and then turned to me. "My queen, I bid you to come into your inner chambers, let me examine you, the child may be on his way."

Before I could disagree with her, I felt the wave of pain come this time settling in my back. I knew she was right; the baby was coming.

As I held onto Anushka on my left, pain blinded me to who was on my right. I walked carefully towards my inner chamber, trying to prepare myself for the hours of pain that were to come. As I walked, I could already feel something firm between my legs, only then did I notice a trail of water behind me. I do not know why I was ashamed; I did not want the king to see me like this. Unlike my first son, this child was in a rush. I screamed with more pain as Anushka set into motion. She set me on the birthing stool and placed her hands between my legs and I cried then rested my back against the wall. The urge to push overwhelmed me and I started to groan and push.

"Wait, wait my queen," Anushka said, her hand still between my legs. "The baby's head rests on my hand, but I feel something tight around his neck."

I let out short sharp breaths, trying to resist the intense urge to push. A cool cloth touched my head bringing blessed relief and a minor distraction from the desire to push that was coursing through my body.

Desperate for moisture, I whispered, "Water." Shortly after, warm honey dripped through my lips. I enjoyed its sweetness for only a moment before pain struck again. I closed my eyes to rest, as a sudden desire to sleep came over me. I felt someone shaking my legs vigorously, forcing me to open my eyes.

Time must have passed, even though it felt like it had somehow stood still as when I opened my eyes, the two midwives who had attended to me the previous year were in the room.

Their voices were raised, and I watched the room fill with people. I turned to see the water basin beside me; it was dark red with many blood-stained cloths on the floor. Before I could consider what was happening, I felt my stomach being massaged firmly. It was painful but I was too weak to scream. A bitter taste filled my mouth, so different from the sweet smell and taste of honey. Another cup was placed on my lips and a hot potion of root of herbs was forced down my throat. I remember the smell of burning metal even though I did not see it until I felt a sharp scratch between my legs and more voices being raised, even though they sounded like mere whispers.

Again, my stomach was pressed. This time, I felt an enormous pressure and two hands between my legs, deep within my womanhood. One pair of hands was pushing my stomach and another was pulling.

The next thing I remember was opening my eyes in a field filled with wildflowers. There I saw a young boy, not more than three or four years old. He looked so familiar; his smile made me smile. I longed to touch him. When I reached out my hand to him, he started to run, and I chased him. Although I had never been here before, it felt safe and familiar, even the air seemed to taste different. I loved the feel of wet earth beneath my feet, and I ran around the field like I was the child. I felt free, like I was floating in the air. When I looked down, I realised my feet were no longer on the ground and I was floating in the air.

The day was brighter than I had ever seen before but when I looked up at the sky, I could not see the sun. Where was I? My curiosity did not give rise to panic, the only emotion I felt was joy. I kept running towards the child; by now he was close enough for me to see him. "David!" I called out to him. The next time I looked, he was older, maybe twelve, not a boy but not quite a man. He smiled down at me, still my arms had not embraced him. I heard my name called, not once, but three times. When I turned, I saw Uriah standing just beyond me, his hand held out to mine. He was dressed in a white tunic that had blue petals on its sleeves. Still, I heard my name was being called. I realised then that it was not Uriah who was calling me. I saw another man dressed in a similar tunic to Uriah's but his was all white and I could not look upon his face. It had no form, just light; it was as though the whole of the field was bright just from his face. It was from him I heard my name being called.

I stood far from the flowers and reached out my hand towards Uriah, but a force separated us. I think it was the light. To my left was Uriah and beyond him was a river and a mountain, they looked like the ones I had seen in my many years before. To my right, a tunnel, inside it was dark. I turned and started walking towards Uriah. With each step I took, he seemed to take a step back, as did the boy. I hastened towards them, but they hurried away. So, I started running. The light moved between us. At first, he did not speak, only pointed towards the tunnel.

I heard my name again. This time I listened. It was called seven times, coming from the tunnel. Now, I recognised the voice: my king; he called my name. I stared from the left to the right. I looked at the mountain and then the tunnel. I had to choose. It seemed my life hung in the balance. I wanted to cry but no tears came. My mind was torn between the mountain and the tunnel. From the tunnel, I heard a baby cry, it was loud and persistent as though it needed food or comfort.

Then I looked towards the light, at the man in the all-white tunic, hoping he would help me decide.

"Go back home, Bathsheba. You have much to do."

Before I had a chance to fight, he raised his right hand and blew a gentle breeze into his palm. It carried me and I floated towards the tunnel. Not trying to fight the wind, I allowed it to move my body forward.

Chapter Forty-Seven

The minute I opened my eyes, a strong pain shot through my body. Every part of me ached like I had been in a battle, beaten with fists. A wet cloth lay on my forehead. The room was quiet but not dark. I lifted myself, trying to find my feet. I could barely move. A thick cloth was stuck between my legs and when I shifted, pain shot through me. I heard the sound of a crying infant in the far distance and my memory returned. My child! Where was my child? I struggled, attempting to look for my baby, but tiredness overtook me. I closed my eyes again, for what I thought was a moment and awakened to a hand on my head. I opened my eyes to see the king and my eyes widened even more.

"My queen." His voice, barely a whisper, was drowned out by the shrieks of the baby in his arms. The king lowered himself to place the baby gently on me. He removed the blanket and placed the child on my bare skin, the infant quietened into gentle sobs as I placed my hand on his back. "Our son," he said, as his lips kissed my forehead, gentle as gossamer as he removed the wet cloth. A boy. Yahweh had blessed me with another boy. I smiled, my heart thankful. Many thoughts ran through my mind as I wondered what I had missed. Why was I in bed in such pain? What happened? My head hurt from trying to remember. Then I looked at the king; he was not supposed to be here. "You are unclean," I said, as though I needed to remind him.

He laughed gently, taking my hand. "If the Lord would take you from me, should the law keep me away from my queen? I wanted to be by your side, Bathsheba. To beg Yahweh for mercy, to return you to me." He took the cloth, placed it in the bowl of cool water and wiped my face with it. "Besides, I have a field full of cattle both young and old, and cages full of birds that I can lay at the feet of the priest." He winked at me, and I managed a smile.

My dream came back to me and I remembered the words of Yahweh. He said I had much to do. I kissed the head of my son now asleep on my chest, then I took the king's hand in mine and brought it to my dry lips. "Yahweh Himself sent me back to you."

He smiled and said, "For that I remain grateful."

I felt a sudden urge to relieve myself so I asked him for the servants to attend to me. He picked up his son and left the inner chambers. When Anushka arrived, she urged me to remain on the bed and instead brought a metal pan to me. At my request, she told me all that happened during the birth. At first, the birth cord was tied around the baby's neck. As she tried to remove it, the baby turned, and his shoulder got stuck. Blood flowed out of me like water and to let the baby come free and stop the bleeding, the midwife had to make a cut in my womanhood, which explained the sharp pain as I emptied my body. Then, she stitched it close when the baby had come forth.

The bitter herbs were given to help the pain but being weak from much bleeding, it put me to sleep. She wept at that point as she said, "My queen, at one time, we thought you were dead. But when we pulled your son out, your breathing returned." She clapped her hands and lifted it like it was an offering. "The boy was placed in Eliana's hands to wash him in salt. I held your legs as the midwives sewed you back, and then we cleansed you. I placed a cloth between your legs. Your son was given to the king at his request, and he wept over the infant. Then, he came to your side, placed a cloth over your head and never left you."

The king returned moments later, dismissing her and placed our son in my arms once more. He cried a little; fussing from being moved from one hand to the other, but when his skin touched mine, he settled again, breathing quietly. I tried to nurse him, but he favoured sleep instead. The boy was as gentle outside me as he was when he was inside. I examined his face closely, enchanted by this miracle. I was not surprised that he looked like his father, but with hair as dark as the night. His skin was clear of any blemish, no freckles, not even a single bruise marred him. I looked at the king and asked, "What shall we call him?"

He pondered for a moment, staring at the infant, then said, "Solomon."

I nodded my acceptance; it was a name well suited to a son who had indeed brought peace.

Chapter Forty-Eight

The King called for seven days of feasting, starting that night. He reminded me that the year before he had fasted for seven days, with deep mourning, but this time, he would rejoice for seven days, praising Yahweh.

The next day, late in the afternoon, I sat nursing my son when the king arrived. The windows were slightly open allowing entry to the loud music which filled the air along with the tantalising smell of roasting lamb. The king stood by the window humming to the tune that blared across the streets of Jerusalem. He remained there for some time, looking out towards the people, watching the merriment happening in his city.

Shortly after, I heard three knocks on the door. The king walked towards it returning with a big velvet box in his hands. I had just finished nursing Solomon and I laid him on his back to sleep. The King placed the box on the bed and then helped me to sit, placing more cushions behind me to give me support. "I have a gift for you, my queen." His eyes twinkled.

"More gifts, my king? What am I to do with all the gold that fills my drawers, the many fabrics and veils? Has the king not done enough already? You have given me much more than I need."

He paid little mind to my comments. Instead, he fiddled with the box trying to open the lock. When he did, he looked inside and I watched as his eyes smiled in approval, as though he was seeing the contents for the first time.

"Can you walk?" he asked.

I nodded. He lifted me off the bed, as I pulled the loose tunic around my body, holding the fastening with one hand and giving him the other. He led me towards the table with the large mirror and gently lowered me on the wooden stool complete with a purple cushion to bring me comfort. I sat right in front of the mirror. As he walked back to retrieve the box, I looked into the mirror and smiled at my reflection; although slightly pale from all the blood I had lost, the bitter herbs that I had been drinking every hour were bringing some colour back to my cheeks. My thick brown hair flowed free around me, falling all the way past my waist. Anushka had spent time that morning brushing it with oil before I placed my crown back on my head.

The king placed the box on the table and said, "Close your eyes." His were wide open, filled with mischief.

I closed mine but not fully; I wanted to see what he was doing.

He placed his palm over my face. "Properly, Bathsheba."

I chuckled then obeyed. My mind started to wonder: what could this gift be in such a large box? The first thing I considered was a necklace. Perhaps he longed to replace the one that had been buried with our first son. Instinctively, my hand went to my neck, touching the place where it used to be. I felt his hand push mine away and when he raised my hair, I expected the cool metal that grazed my neck.

"Open your eyes."

I did his bidding and saw the beautiful necklace he had placed around my neck. Hanging on a gold chain was a single leaf with precious red and green stones set around it. I loved it. I placed my hand on the rough pendant, enjoying the feel of the stones and mindlessly counted them. Then I looked at the unopened box confused.

Again, he said, "Close your eyes."

This time I did not argue or question him, I simply closed my eyes tight, not even moving when I heard Solomon cry softly. I felt the crown on my head being lifted by the king. I panicked, desperate to open my eyes to witness the moment I was being dethroned. Then I heard the box open and the King placed something on my head: it had more weight. "Open your eyes, my love," he whispered into my ear. I liked the sound of his words; it was the first time he had ever called me that name; one he had insisted that I called him. I smiled as I opened my eyes and saw the most beautiful crown ever made.

"It sits well on you, my queen" and he kissed my cheek, his lips lingering sensually.

I shivered at his touch.

I stared at it for a long moment, taking in every detail. It was at least three times bigger than the one I had already. It had more stones than I could ever imagine. On top of each of its twelve spikes was a large pearl and on each pearl was a white stone.

Each of the twelve spikes also had precious stones down the length of it alongside tiny pearls. It had golden threads that intertwined the spikes and curved unto the base. To say it was beautiful would betray its true description. I touched it gently, carefully; I could not take my eyes off it.

The King walked towards the bed and picked up Solomon who was now awake crying. He rocked the baby and returned to my side. Leaning towards me, he pulled a bench with his foot and then he sat beside me placing the infant in my arms. He quietened.

"It appears my son favours you over me," he teased.

I turned towards him. "Another crown?" I asked, tears pouring down my cheeks. I had never known any queen to have more than one crown; it was not like the numerous bangles or rings we often got as gifts. I remembered when I first sat at the king's Sabbath meal, the first one since I entered the palace, I noticed with sadness my crown was unlike the others — it was simple. It did not trouble me much because of the two doves that sat on either side of mine. That was symbolic to me, a constant reminder of my vision and the hand of Yahweh in my predicament. But now, as I stared at my new crown, I knew it was the most beautiful in the palace, bearing much likeness to the king's own crown.

"Why, my king?" I asked, grateful and confused in equal measure.

He placed his arms around me. "This crown is befitting of the mother of the heir to my throne, the mother of the future king."

No words came to my mouth. I tasted the salty tears, wiping the drops that had fallen on Solomon's head. The one who takes, is truly the one who gives and my Yahweh had given me much more than He had taken.

Even though I had been married to the king for two years, a part of me never felt like I truly belonged. I sometimes felt like a stranger with the constant fear that I would be cast aside one day. But for the first time, right then, in that moment, in the arms of my love, as I recalled the words he spoke. I stared at my reflection in the mirror with the reigning King sitting on my right and the future king nestled in my arms, my heart completely welcomed the truth – I had become Queen Bathsheba.

I thought my joy would be short-lived when three loud knocks came on the door and we welcomed the servant with the news that caused my blood to immediately run cold. The prophet Nathan had summoned the King.

When the king left for his throne room, a tray of food, full to overflowing with a variety of fruits, watered wine, roasted lamb, fresh vegetables, cakes, bread, and a large cup with the bitter root herbs, was brought to me. I took my time to note everything on the tray looking at the food items for distraction after which I pushed it to one side, choosing to nurse Solomon instead. He suckled too quickly and started choking on the milk. Although my heart started to beat faster and panic tingled at my nerve ends, I quickly placed him on his chest and patted his back much harder than the occasion demanded.

"Be at peace, my queen," was all Anushka said before she carefully lifted the baby from my hands, replacing it with the cup of herbs.

"Peace?" I spat the words out. "Did your ears not hear that the Prophet Nathan has summoned the king?" Without waiting for her response, I climbed into the middle of my bed and covered my head completely with the blanket. Why did I not go to the mountain? Why would Yahweh send me into the tunnel to come and suffer another season of tears? My heart barely survived a year ago; I knew I could not go through the pain again. "Yahweh, please, have mercy on me. Please have mercy on us," I cried out loud, calling on my God.

A few moments later, I heard the sandals of the king as he approached. I held my breath but could still hear my heartbeat loud in my ears. He walked towards the bed, uncovered me, and climbed in next to me. My eyes remained closed but my ears waited to hear the news. I could feel the King's breath near me, but he spoke no words, merely stroking my face. I waited a moment more and it was not until I felt his lips gently touch mine that I dared to open my eyes to his smile. "The prophet brings good news, my queen."

My body relaxed. "The prophet says that our son has been given a new name from God. He is *Jedidiah* because he is beloved of the Lord" As I rested in his arms, I wept with joy praising Yahweh from the depths of my soul.

Epilogue

I place the pen down and stretch my body. The hours have moved by so quickly. Several sheets of paper stare at me, wet from ink. Who will read my story? I ponder. After many hours of writing, my fingers are weak and tender to the touch. My stomach growls, gently reminding me that I have eaten little but worked endlessly, only pausing to feed and clean Solomon.

I enjoy caring for him myself, though the palace is filled with many open arms willing to care for him. I trust him with only two – Anushka and Eliana, and both often complain that I do not place the baby in their arms enough. If I let them, they will hold him all day and night.

The king has still not returned from state duties and darkness settles well into the night. I wipe the tears that flow with the corner of my sleeve. The memories feel raw and fresh as though they happened only yesterday. I place down the pen. I am satisfied, enough has been said for now, though there is much more hidden in my soul. Grief is a persistent emotion, and time doesn't heal it, Yahweh does, and He does it well. His healing does not erase the memories; it replaces the pain with comfort. For this, I am grateful. I don't ever want to forget my past as there are too many lessons to be learned.

I know that in my lifetime, many other women will fall victim to the trials I suffered in my past - being taken against their will. We live in a society that sees a free woman only slightly better than a slave but never as equal to a man. Women have no voice, no choice, only submission to whoever is master over them. But what I have seen with my own eyes and experienced through my own pain is that Yahweh is unlike any man. He is one who is everywhere, He sees everything, and He brings justice. Although each man has a right to choose of his own free will, each choice comes with a consequence and the consequences of bad choices can be painful and extend for generations to come.

When the king told me the truth of what the prophet Nathan said, in much more detail than my Saba did, I wept from the depths of my soul. He told me the word of the prophet said — the sword will never depart from the house of King David. Adversity will rise up within his own house and his wives will be taken by others in the presence of all. His sin was in secret but theirs will be in the open and the last consequence, the one that grieved my soul almost to the point of death, was the death of our first son. We all, each of us have to count the cost and weigh from the beginning to the end the impact of our decisions. Will it bring God praise or bring us ruin? We must think.

The truth is, the body will demand much from us, at a cost that our spirit will be unwilling to pay; we cannot give room for our own ways. This truth is one of many I hope to teach my sons. The one I turn to look at and the one that rests in my stomach, I cannot wait to share the news with the King tonight. Excited, I place my hands on my belly and rub it gently, grateful to Yahweh. The one who takes is the one who gives, and He has given me much more than was taken away. There is joy for my pain and purpose ahead of me.

I walk over to the basket and pick up the crying Solomon who, surprisingly, is hungry again. He has grown quickly, spending a lot of his waking hours running, then falling and also putting everything his hand can touch in his mouth. He nurses and goes back to sleep. The night is fully upon us, the sky is star-filled and I see fireflies dancing just outside the window.

He stirs in my arms, his eyes closed but his body demands my attention. I look at him, he is a miracle in my arms, a son I did not expect to hold, a son that already has purpose placed on his head.

True to his name, Solomon is filled with peace. He is a treasure to mother, crying little except for food or with discomfort. His smile steals the heart of everyone who sees him on earth and even the one who sent him from heaven, the one who called him His beloved.

I do not know what the future holds but I wait for it with much anticipation, shifting under the weight of the responsibility that I carry in my arms.

In the last year the prophet Nathan has become more than a voice from the Lord. He is a counsellor, a mentor, and a trusted friend. I have learnt much from him. I am grateful to Yahweh that I have the ear of the prophet as I know that I am going to need all the support, wisdom, direction and prayers that I can get for the mammoth task ahead of me — raising the next King of Israel.

The End

Glossary

- *Abba* - God as father
- *Adonai* - A Hebrew word that means My Lord
- *Mikveh* - A ritual bath in which various Jewish purifications are performed
- *Niddah* - A woman who has experienced a uterine discharge of blood (most commonly during menstruation)
- *Saba* - Grandfather in Hebrew
- *Sheloshim* - the thirty days of mourning
- *Shiva* - the seven days of mourning
- *Yahweh* - A Hebrew name for God

Author's Note

Firstly, I must state clearly – most parts of this novel are a work of pure fiction.

The story of King David and Bathsheba is one that has always left me feeling a bit unsettled. If you haven't read the story recently, can I suggest you take some time to read 2 Samuel 11-12 as it will help you understand my notes and why I have written the story in the way that I have.

For many years, I wrestled with the need to tell it from another point of view. There have been movies, books, articles, and various teachings about this particular story. The majority of them have one thing in common — they rationalise the events that occurred and usually call it adultery.

Other well-known Bible fiction authors have written this story with that same principle in mind. Some have suggested Bathsheba always liked David. Another book I read alluded to the fact that Bathsheba was bored, and this led to an uncanny seduction of the king. However the story is told, the outcome is always the same, somehow, Bathsheba contributed to the reason she was defiled. After all, she was naked near a window.

Doesn't it sound like the same story we hear even today? 'Her skirt was too short.' 'Why was she out alone at night?' 'She said no, but her body was saying yes...'

It is one of those stories that is difficult to imagine and accept at face value and I think it is because of who we know David is — a man after God's own heart. How can somebody so good do something so bad? I get that, and to be honest, I struggled with that as well.

But then I had a real burden for Bathsheba, one that I have carried for years. Can we stop and imagine the possibility that she was a woman, happily married to her husband, minding her own business when she was summoned by the most powerful man at that time and taken against her will?

She ends up pregnant and is forced to marry the man who defiled her and murdered her husband in cold blood. Can you even begin to imagine what that must have been like for her?

I have written this story purely from the Bible's perspective and there is nothing in the Bible that remotely alludes to the fact that there was any type of previous relationship or consent given, so no, it was not adultery.

I have read commentaries that suggest she should have screamed; she should have refused. Could she? This was a time when women had absolutely no voice. Even if she did scream, who would have come to her rescue, what difference would it have made?

Queen Esther had to ask for three days of prayer and fasting before she could appear before her own husband King Xerxes uninvited, knowing it would cost her, her life (see Esther 5). King David's only daughter Tamar was raped by her own brother. She screamed, she begged, it made no difference whatsoever (see 2 Samuel 13).

If Bathsheba was in anyway complicit, why did God only punish David? The Prophet Nathan was quite clear. The consequences of David's sin were great; not only did it lead to the death of the child but there were generational implications too. We see the evidence of this shortly after with the rape of Tamar in 2 Samuel 13.

There are many sad parts to this story but one that pulls at my heart is when God says to David in 2 Samuel 12:8 NIV - "I gave your master's house to you, and your master's wives into your arms. I gave you all Israel and Judah. *And if all this had been too little, I would have given you even more*" (italics mine). I think this is one of the saddest parts of scripture; it challenges me and reminds me that God is willing to give us more than what we need if we do things the right way.

Another bit that leaves me in pieces is Uriah's death. This was a man who was clearly a good man, a loyal man, a member of the King's inner circle. He was one of the King's Thirty elite soldiers. This man was so loyal to the king and his job that he refused to go home to his wife, and it was this loyalty that cost him his life. His own hands carried the message that contained the order for his death. That is sad on so many levels.

However, let us imagine that Uriah did go home. David's attempt at paternity fraud would have worked. The son of the king would have been raised in the house of his servant. The bigger lesson here is that this whole concept of paternity fraud is not new. There are many families that have suffered the pain associated with this type of deception. It is a reminder that many women who have had to endure this fate don't always do it from a position of promiscuity; sometimes they find themselves in very difficult and painful situations without their control. Paternity fraud has caused so many issues in Africa with many families torn apart. Perhaps we can learn to be a bit more understanding, knowing things are not always what they seem.

My purpose in writing this novel is not to make David out as a bad guy, far from it. David has always and will continue to be one of my favourite Bible heroes. The lesson to learn here is that good people can do some very bad things but where there is true repentance with God, it can work out for good. However, we must know that there will be consequences for our bad decisions and most times they can be life changing so we need to think before we act.

I love that God did not withhold justice even to the one He loved, and it gives me comfort and reassurance that we serve a God who sees everything. I hope that this will bring comfort to many women who have been wounded by men in authority as even today, there are women who still suffer from the hands of men who have some kind of control or authority over them. Sadly, that same culture still exists today. The 'me-too' movement has shown us that there are men in power that still take advantage of women today.

I decided to write this novel in first person as I truly wanted to capture Bathsheba's point of view in detail. I wanted to bring her emotions alive and give her the voice that she lost in a culture that brought her pain. I pray that many women will find comfort in this story.

As someone who was sexually abused as a child, I know that this is one of the stories that has encouraged me and reminded me that God can take painful circumstances and turn them around for good. God can also use women who have been broken to serve his eternal purposes. God used Bathsheba in a powerful way.

The chronology of Jesus in the Book of Matthew shows us Joseph's lineage all the way back to Solomon. However, there is another chronology in the Bible, it is found in the book of Luke, and it shows a lineage all the way back to Nathan. At first, this may appear to be a contradiction in the Bible, but many scholars have now stated that the genealogy in Matthew is Joseph's and the one in Luke is Mary's.

Bathsheba is the mother of both Solomon and Nathan. If what the Bible scholars say is true, this means that she is the only woman in the Bible that has a double claim to the lineage of Jesus: how awesome is that? God used a woman like her to change history. This also shows that Jesus was truly and fully a son of David, with a lineage that runs both from His mother and father's side all the way back to Bathsheba.

In writing this novel, I did a lot of research, read a lot of articles and books, and read the Bible with every single reference to this story from the Book of Samuel and Kings. It is from this research that I have included key aspects of this story, i.e., King David promising Bathsheba that Solomon will be King after Him (1Kings 1:17) Also, the Bible does not state that King David had any other wife after Bathsheba and in his old age, the concubine Abishag only serves to keep him warm (1 Kings 1). This is why I wrote the novel to end as a love story, to bring hope and joy.

The Bible also suggests that there was a good relationship formed between Bathsheba and the Prophet Nathan as he is the one that advises her on what to do and say to King David when he finds out that another of his sons wanted to ascend the throne (1 Kings 1:11-14). There have been suggestions that Nathan became a mentor to Bathsheba and her third son was named after him.

I hope that you enjoyed reading this novel as much as I enjoyed writing it. I hope that it blessed you and that you found joy and comfort in her story. This is a love story that started with pain and bitterness but then takes you on a journey with Bathsheba as she evolves from servant to queen.

I would love to hear your thoughts so please connect with me on social media.

www.amandabedzrah.com

About the Author

Amanda Bedzrah is an award-winning author, with much of her work grounded in the redeeming, empowering and transformative power of God's love. Her debut book, *The Love That Set Me Free* was met with critical acclaim, with readers recognising themselves — and finding healing — through her autobiographical account of childhood abuse, suppression and trauma.

Since then, she has authored several instructional guides for living life fully according to God's will including *5 Habits of Godly Resilient Women*, *Overcoming the Fear of Death*, and Praying *Proverbs*. She has also designed and published 2 Journals for developing the art of kindness.

Becoming Queen Bathsheba is her second piece of Christian fiction, following on from the successful *Leah*. It is set to become another bestseller in a series of novels based on Women in the Bible.

When she is not writing, speaking, teaching the Bible or coaching, Amanda can be found desperately searching for the next quaint coffee house in which to curl up with a book.

facebook.com/amandabedzrah

twitter.com/gigidoll2020

instagram.com/Amanda_Bedzrah

Also by Amanda Bedzrah

Fiction

Leah: Unnoticed. Unwanted. Unloved

Non – Fiction

The Love that set me free

Overcoming the fear of death

Praying Proverbs

5 Habits of Godly Resilient Women

My Super Power is Kindness (A Journal for Kids)

Choosing Kindness Everyday (A Journal for Teenage Girls & Women)

An Introduction to Women in the Bible